This copy of

THE SECRET OF LOST LAKE
by Carolyn Keene

belongs to

_____

_____

Other Sparrow Books by Carolyn Keene

Carolyn Keene

THE SECRET OF LOST LAKE

SPARROW
BOOKS

A Sparrow Book
Published by Arrow Books Limited
17-21 Conway Street, London W1P 6JD

An imprint of the Hutchinson Publishing Group

London Melbourne Sydney Auckland
Johannesburg and agencies
throughout the world

First published in Great Britain 1983

Made and printed in Great Britain
by The Anchor Press Ltd
Tiptree, Essex

ISBN 0 09 931300 6

CONTENTS

CHAPTER I

A Missing Baron

THE diesel engines strained a little on the Rocky Mountain grade, as Louise and Jean Dana gazed in fascination from the train compartment at the abruptly changing landscape.

"This area," said the slender, bespectacled gentleman seated opposite them, "is dinosaur country."

"Do you mean those mammoth prehistoric reptiles lived here?" asked Miss Harriet Dana, the girls' aunt, who was traveling East with them.

"Yes, they roamed all over this place," said Professor Cary Nesbitt, curator at a San Francisco museum. The girls had met him recently. "No one is sure why they died out, but one theory is that the glaciers overpowered them. Dinosaurs were pretty dumb creatures—their brains were very small compared to their seventy-foot-long bodies and twenty-ton weight."

Jean grinned. "Tall reptiles for tall mountains! How I'd love to find some fossil bones!"

The conversation in the closed compartment was interrupted by a low bark. It came from a handsome German shepherd dog lying on the floor at their feet. The Danas had received special permission to keep him with them.

"What's the matter, Baron?" Louise asked him. "Tired of being shut in here? Well, next time the train stops we'll go for a run."

She explained to the professor, who had come from another car to visit, that Baron Otto von Neckar was a famous show dog. The girls were taking him to his new owner in New York.

Aunt Harriet sighed. "I'll be glad when the responsibility is over and we can go home. Thanksgiving will soon be here," she said, looking out at the patches of snow on the ranchlands and distant mountains.

Jean asked the professor to tell them more about the countryside. The tall, distinguished-looking man smiled. "The area south of here is full of mystery."

Instantly the girls were alert. More than anything else, seventeen-year-old, brunette Louise and her blond sister, a year younger, enjoyed solving mysteries. From the time of their first case, *Mystery of the Stone Tiger*, to their recent one, *The Sierra Gold Mystery*, the Danas had been involved in challenging mysteries.

"What kind of mysteries?" Louise asked.

"Well, the most interesting to me concerns Lost Lake. Once there was a—"

At this instant the train came to a sudden, jarring halt. The compartment door flew open and baggage shifted about. Baron gave a yelp of pain. Jean found herself in Professor Nesbitt's lap, while Louise collided with Aunt Harriet.

Quickly the group disentangled itself and Miss Dana asked, "Is everyone all right?" They confessed to being shaken, and Jean and the professor had bruises from having bumped into each other. But otherwise the four travellers were all right.

From the forward car came groans and cries for help.

"Perhaps we can give some first aid," Louise suggested. "Let's go and see."

Professor Nesbitt decided to return to his own car to help and said good-bye.

At that very moment Jean cried out, "Baron is gone!"

Aunt Harriet looked worried. "Oh, dear, I hope he didn't get scared and run away. I'll never forgive myself if that valuable dog is lost!"

Louise began to call and whistle for Baron. He did not come. Thinking the dog might be in another car, she and her sister hurried to the end of the car. The outer door stood open.

"Baron probably went outside," Jean said. She hurried down the steps and looked around. The dog was not in sight. She called him several times but Baron did not appear.

"Look!" said Louise, joining her sister. "I see dog prints in that patch of snow!"

The marks were unmistakable—freshly made prints. How far away did they lead?

"What'll we do?" asked Jean. "If we follow them, the train might pull out before we get back, and we'd be stranded."

"But losing Baron—" Louise began, then said, "Let's go forward and find out what happened and exactly when the train will leave."

By this time most of the passengers had come outside and were milling about, talking excitedly. Louise and Jean learned from the conductor that a journal on the first engine had overheated and burned off, ripping up part of the track.

"Fortunately, no one was seriously injured," the conductor stated. "A doctor on board is attending to a few with minor injuries and hysteria."

"I'm glad the wreck was no worse," said Louise. "How long do you think we'll be here?"

"We've sent for a wrecking crew, but it'll be several hours before we can pull out," the conductor said. "Help's coming from Green River."

Louise explained about the lost dog and said the girls would like to search for him.

"Okay, but be back within four hours," the trainman advised.

The sisters hurried to tell Aunt Harriet. After hearing their plan, she said, "All right. But I'm going with you."

She and the girls put on warm coats and walking shoes. As they left the train, Jean remarked that Baron's prints led south. The three Danas had no trouble following them through one patch of snow after another.

Part of the way led through comparatively flat land with sheep grazing in the distance. The crisp, clear air afforded a long view ahead. Baron was not in sight. The girls called and whistled, thinking the dog might be lying down or even drinking in an irrigation ditch. He failed to respond.

The tracks led up and down a hill, which Louise and Jean climbed, while Miss Dana skirted the base. Her nieces waited until she joined them. All sat down to rest.

"What do you think was in Baron's mind?" Jean asked.

"Freedom," Aunt Harriet answered. "There are no other animal tracks, so he wasn't after a rabbit or a squirrel, and none of the Rocky Mountain lions was bothering him."

Louise shuddered at the last remark. Baron might be able to defend himself, but he might be scarred or incapacitated, so he could never be a show dog again!

"Shall we go?" Jean urged.

The three arose and trekked on. After an hour's walk they saw a ranch house nestled at the foot of a small mountain.

"Baron's tracks lead right to it!" Jean cried out excitedly. "We've found him!"

Louise and Aunt Harriet were excited, too, but not so positive as Jean. Nevertheless, all three hurried toward the ranch house. A dog began to bark a warning of their approach.

"That's not Baron," Louise stated.

As she spoke, a large white sheep dog bounded toward the Danas. "Hello, old girl!" Jean said in greeting. "Where's your master?"

Discovering that the callers were friendly, the dog led them to the kitchen door of the house. It opened and a smiling, weather-beaten man of sixty stepped out. His hair had the slightest hint of grey and his smile of welcome was warm.

"I reckon you folks were in that train wreck," he said. "Heard it over the radio. But if you don't mind telling me, what made you take such a long walk?"

"My goodness, John Strong," said a woman behind him, "why don't you invite the folks in? They're probably about ready to drop."

Mr. Strong chuckled heartily. "You're right, Martha. I'm forgetting my manners entirely. Please come in!"

He stepped aside, revealing a small, pretty woman his age. After the Danas introduced themselves to the Strongs, the ranchwoman ushered her callers through the large kitchen, with its shiny copper kettles hanging on the walls and a table covered with a red-checkered cloth.

The group entered a pleasant living room. Here the pine-panelled walls, beamed ceiling, wide-board floor, and comfortable furniture gave the room a cozy, welcoming atmosphere.

Mrs. Strong immediately brought in a pot of coffee and served it with homemade cookies, biscuits, and jelly. "Tell us about the wreck," she said.

"Before we do that," Louise spoke up, "we want to tell you why we're here. A valuable German shepherd dog we were taking to New York ran away. We think we traced his paw prints here. Did you see him?"

"Indeed we did," Mr. Strong answered. "Was that your dog? Too bad we didn't tie him up."

"We fed him," Mrs. Strong broke in. "You know it's bad luck not to feed an animal that comes to you."

Her husband laughed. "That's just another one of your superstitions, Martha. We'll show you folks our menagerie of helpless animals that came here—my wife's pets."

In the ensuing conversation with the Strongs it became apparent that they were a fine, lovable couple and also that the rancher was somewhat amused by his wife's superstitious fears.

"Have you any idea where Baron—our dog—went?" Louise asked finally.

Mr. Strong pointed directly south. "He was headed straight for wild country."

"Is that in the direction of Lost Lake?" Jean asked.

"Yes. Exactly."

The Danas groaned. "He'll be swallowed up in the wilderness!" Jean declared. "Where would we start looking for him?"

Aunt Harriet asked worriedly, "What will we ever tell Baron's old and new owners? This is terrible!"

Mrs. Strong nodded her head sympathetically, but added the electrifying remark, "I only hope that the witch of Lost Lake doesn't get hold of Baron!"

CHAPTER II

Sleuthing on Horseback

AFTER the initial shock of Mrs. Strong's statement, Louise asked, "Did you say the witch of Lost Lake?"

"Yes," the rancher's wife replied. "You mentioned Lost Lake yourself. You've never heard of the witch who lives there?"

All the Danas turned toward Mr. Strong as if to inquire, "Is this another one of your wife's superstitious fears?"

He must have guessed their thoughts because he said with a smile, "Martha is not making up the story. Would you like to hear all about Lost Lake?"

"Indeed we would," Jean spoke up. "A professor on the train told us there was a mystery connected with it. Before he could go on, the wreck occurred and we never heard the rest of the story."

Mr. Strong, who had been standing up all this time drinking his coffee, now seated himself.

"About forty years ago there was a large beautiful lake which the Indians of this region used in some kind of religious ceremonial. When white men moved into the area, they built up a small but thriving community. One day there was an earthquake which caused a great landslide of the mountain bordering the east side of the lake. That's where the town was located. It was almost wiped out—not a soul left alive."

"How dreadful!" Miss Dana murmured.

"You said no one survived," Louise spoke up. "Then how does this witch fit in?"

Mr. Strong said that a young woman of the community had been in New York at the time of the disaster. "Or rather, she had been in New York and was on her way home. When she arrived, she was confronted with the utter desolation of the catastrophe and, of course, the death of her parents.

"From the stories I've heard, she was a very lovely young girl, but the shock of the tragedy unnerved her completely. It's rumoured she refused to leave the place and became sort of a recluse.

"People in town say she's a little peculiar, and has been for a good many years. She only comes to town when it's necessary to buy supplies or perhaps get another horse. She never talks to anyone and pays for what she buys with Indian artifacts which she digs up."

"Imagine living out there all alone!" Jean shuddered. "How can she stand it?"

"No one knows," Mrs. Strong put in. "Some people say she has supernatural powers—that's how she got the name of witch. We've never heard her right name. Folks in town always refer to her as the witch of Lost Lake."

Louise and Jean felt that there probably was some other reason why the witch stayed on at the deserted place. Surely her grief alone would not have kept her there.

"I wonder what her secret is," Louise thought.

Miss Dana asked if the original lake had vanished.

"Not entirely," the rancher answered. "One small corner of it has remained. The river into which it flowed disappeared, but a new small stream opened up at the opposite end."

"I'd certainly like to meet the witch," said Jean eagerly.

Aunt Harriet reminded her nieces that this would be impossible. "We must start back to the train. It is unfortunate having to leave Baron behind, but we can do nothing more."

Suddenly Mrs. Strong smiled and said, "If you could possibly postpone going home, John and I would love to have you Danas stay here. Reports are for good weather. You could use some of our horses and make a further search for Baron."

"That would be marvellous!" Jean exclaimed. She looked pleadingly toward Aunt Harriet. "Oh, please accept the invitation," she begged.

Miss Dana was thoughtful. She did not want to impose on these good-natured people, yet she too had a great desire to retrieve the valuable German shepherd dog.

Mr. Strong spoke up. "I think Martha's idea is an excellent one. When you are ready to leave here, I could drive you to Green River to catch a train for New York."

"Aunt Harriet," said Louise, "we could postpone going home for another week or so. School won't open until after Thanksgiving, you know, so we have time."

There had been a serious fire at Starhurst School which the sisters attended, and classes had been suspended since early October. Students had been given assignments for weeks in advance and the Danas had faithfully studied theirs.

"Well, I do appreciate the invitation," Miss Dana finally said. "But before accepting, I *would* like to know more about what we'll be running into if we try to search for Baron."

The rancher smiled. "There's no use beating around the bush. This is rugged country, with many wild animals prowling about. Incidentally, it is reported that the witch is very handy with a rifle. She's a dead shot hitting wild animals that come to bother her."

Louise and Jean closed their eyes for a moment as if to shut out the sight of the witch's mistaking

Baron for a wild animal and aiming at him. Louise told herself, "That's all the more reason we should hunt for the dog before it's too late!"

"If we do stay," Aunt Harriet went on, "we'll have to go back to the train and pick up our luggage. We could walk there, but we couldn't return with all those heavy bags."

"I'll soon fix that up," said Mr. Strong. "Are you girls used to horseback riding?"

"Oh, yes," they replied.

"Then," said the rancher, "you can each ride a horse to the train and take a pack horse with you to carry your luggage."

"You're sure it will be perfectly safe for the girls to go alone?" Miss Dana asked uneasily.

"Oh, yes," he replied cheerily. "You walked here and didn't see anything to bother you."

Miss Dana admitted this was true and gave her consent for the girls to make the trip. "But be careful," she cautioned.

Mrs. Strong spoke up. "You can't go in those rigs. Come with me and I'll find you some Levis and boots."

The rancher's wife explained that the Strongs had a daughter who was now married and living in Seattle. Her mother had kept all her riding clothes. "They come in mighty handy whenever we have visitors," the ranchwoman added, smiling.

"You are extremely kind," Louise told her.

Mrs. Strong laughed. "I guess that's partly because I love animals so much. It hurts me to think of that beautiful shepherd dog being lost in the mountains. I want to do everything I can to help you find him."

After the girls had changed their clothes, they walked to the corral with Mr. Strong. He chose two gentle, well-mannered, sure-footed mares for them. Louise's, he said, was named Ginger. She was a copper palomino and very pretty. He brought out Jubilee, a sleek chestnut quarter horse for Jean.

The girls mounted, and after they had ridden around the corral several times until they felt adjusted to the saddles and the horses' gaits, the rancher led out a pack horse and handed the lead rope to Louise. The girls waved and started off.

By following Baron's paw marks and their own footprints, they were able to reach the train in a comparatively short time. Louise dismounted, and while Jean held Ginger, she went to find the conductor. Louise explained to him what the Danas intended to do and gave her name and that of the Strongs so they could be notified in case Baron returned to the train. She was amused by the look of utter astonishment that came over the conductor's face.

"I call that fast planning," he said at last, laughing. "I think we can pick up some people at Denver to take your compartment. Send your tickets to the railroad company and you will receive a refund."

When Louise rejoined her sister, she found that several passengers had come up to Jean, including Professor Nesbitt. The ones who had not known the girls on the train mistook them for local ranch inhabitants. A couple of young men began to tease the Danas and would not believe they had been travelling on the train until Professor Nesbitt assured them the sisters were telling the truth.

"Well, how about my going back with you?" one red-haired, grinning youth asked. "I could ride on that extra horse."

"Sorry," said Jean, returning his grin, "but our baggage is going to ride on that horse!" The young man pretended to be crushed.

Professor Nesbitt and two other passengers helped the Danas carry their luggage to the pack horse and strap it on. When everything was ready, the kindly museum curator said good-by for a second time.

"I wish I could accompany you girls and hunt for dinosaur fossils. It would be very exciting. But I have a couple of lectures to give in Denver. Well, best of luck and I hope you find Baron."

"Thank you," said Louise. "I certainly hope we do. Anyway, we'll let you know!"

"Please do." The professor smiled, waving as the Danas moved off.

Louise, still guiding the pack horse, was not able to go very fast. But Jubilee, evidently tired of walking slowly, suddenly began to lope. Her young rider did not try to stop the horse.

"This is fun!" Jean thought.

She gave Jubilee her head. Then, suddenly, too late to pull the horse around, she saw a deep hole. Jubilee stepped into it and Jean flew off the mare's back!

CHAPTER III

Sinister Carvings

JEAN DANA lay dazed from the fall. Jubilee struggled out of the hole into which her right front leg had stumbled.

In a few seconds Louise, who had dropped the pack horse's lead rope, ground-hitching it, raced up. She dismounted and leaned over her sister. "Jean! Jean! Are you— How do you feel?"

Jean opened her eyes, blinked, and then managed a faint smile.

"I'm—all—right, I guess," she said, sitting up slowly. Then, recalling what had happened, she asked anxiously, "How's Jubilee? Oh, I hope she didn't break a leg!"

She got up and the two girls walked over to the horse. Jean hugged Jubilee. "Don't worry," she said soothingly. "I'm not angry. The accident wasn't your fault. Oh, I only hope you're all right!"

Louise led the mare around and watched the horse's legs as she walked.

"Jubilee's limping only a little," Louise said finally. "I guess she isn't badly hurt."

"Thank goodness," said Jean, relieved. "Just the same, I'll walk her in."

"Oh, no, you don't," Louise said firmly. "You had a mean tumble. You ride Ginger and I'll lead Jubilee back to the ranch."

Jean did not object. She now gazed at the hole into which her horse had stepped. "Some animal made that, I suppose," she remarked.

Louise helped her sister climb into Ginger's saddle. The girls watched carefully for further holes, and arrived safely at the ranch house.

Mr. Strong came out to meet them. When the rancher heard what had happened, he examined Jubilee's leg thoroughly.

"Some liniment will soon fix that up," he said, relieved. "We'll let the horse rest for a day and she'll be as good as ever."

When the Danas' baggage had been unloaded from the pack horse, Aunt Harriet insisted that Jean take it easy. Her niece agreed reluctantly, but hated to give up the search for Baron.

"Maybe he'll come back tonight," Louise said encouragingly.

During supper, which consisted of a delicious lamb stew and freshly baked applesauce cake with vanilla sauce, Mr. Strong said, "If Baron doesn't come back here by tomorrow morning, how would you girls like to go with me on a day's hunt for him?"

"That would be terrific!" Jean said enthusiastically.

Louise smiled. "You know we'd love to, but can you spare the time?"

The rancher gave a hearty laugh. "I'll take time. This is an important assignment, isn't it?" he asked.

"We think so," Louise replied.

Talk turned again to the witch of Lost Lake.

"What does she look like?" Jean asked.

"We've never seen her," Mrs. Strong replied, "but we understand she has long grey hair. She always wears men's clothes and hats, so you can imagine what a strange picture she makes when she goes to town."

"I feel very sorry for her," Louise murmured.

It was decided that Mr. Strong and the girls would start off early the next morning and take a lunch with them. By ten o'clock that night everyone was sound asleep.

Although the Danas slept well, they did awaken several times during the night hoping that some sound they had heard might be the whine or bark of the missing German shepherd dog. But the sun arose without a visit from Baron.

When breakfast was over, the girls dressed for the trip and went out to the corral. Mr. Strong had three horses saddled, a Tennessee walker named Rondy for Jean, Ginger for Louise, and his white-nosed bay quarter horse. Lunches were put into the saddlebags and the three riders mounted.

The friendly ranch dog whined and danced around. Mr. Strong smiled. "Sorry, Eleanor," he said, "but we can't take you this time. You're a good detective, though. Keep that nose of yours sniffing for any sign of Baron."

He and the girls waved good-by to Aunt Harriet and Mrs. Strong, then started off. It was easy to follow Baron's tracks in the patches of light snow that lay scattered on the rolling landscape. The riders went on and on over grazing land, through wooded areas where golden aspen leaves danced in the sun, and in and out of glacier-gouged canyons with colourful candy-striped cliffs. About an hour later the riders reached a wind-swept canyon bench. Here there was no snow and the tracks disappeared completely.

"Now what are we going to do?" Louise asked in disappointment.

"We could skirt this bench, I suppose," said Mr. Strong, rubbing his chin thoughtfully. "It will take quite a while, though. Too long to try today. Since we're here, I suggest you investigate a very interesting cave. It's not far."

"You mean the formation is interesting?" Jean asked.

"No, it's what is inside. The Indians left some petroglyphs on the cave walls. They're kind of amusing—and instructive."

"Did the Indians of this territory do much carving in stone?" Louise inquired.

"A good bit, yes," Mr. Strong replied. "They also painted pictographs by using paint made from ocher. Of course the petroglyphs chipped from the stone are far better preserved."

It took almost two hours to reach the cave and Jean thought in amusement, "These Western 'side trips' would just about cover a small state back East!"

The riders dismounted and ground-hitched their horses. Mr. Strong led the way into the wide-mouthed cave. As he entered, the rancher turned on a powerful flashlight which he had taken from his saddlebag.

"What a sight!" Louise cried out.

"It's fantastic!" Jean exclaimed.

The rock walls were covered with figures, most of them about half the size of the person or animal which each represented. Mr. Strong focused his flashlight on a group of mountain goats and antelope. Near them were two stalking hunters.

With a grin the rancher remarked, "I'd say those ancient Indians ate well!"

"Yes, and also were cruel fighters," Louise observed, pausing before a fierce-looking warrior.

"Here's a funny one," Jean pointed out as Mr.

Strong played the beam of the flashlight along the cave walls. "This fellow must have been an ancient astronaut!"

Rising from the head of the man were three narrow lines that looked like antennas. At the top of one of these was a circle resembling a balloon.

"I wonder how far he could fly," Louise said, giggling.

"This figure might represent an ancient god," said Mr. Strong. "As you probably know, there are all sorts of legends about Indian gods that came to them from space or from across the water."

"Then you think this one might be arriving from some other planet?" Louise asked.

"Yes."

Mr. Strong turned and beamed his light on the wall near the left side of the entrance. The sightseers stared in astonishment.

Chipped out of the rock was the figure of an elderly woman with long hair. She was leaning over, as if about to pick up something from the ground.

"That's new!" cried Mr. Strong in amazement. "It wasn't here the last time I visited this cave."

"Do you suppose," Louise asked excitedly, "that it's meant to portray the witch of Lost Lake?"

Before the rancher could answer her, his flashlight revealed another recently carved figure which had been chipped a short distance from the woman. It was crudely done, probably because the sculptor's tool had broken. Part of it lay on the ground. The scene depicted a man with a shovel sneaking up behind the woman as if about to strike her!

"How gruesome!" Jean exclaimed.

Mr. Strong's brow furrowed. "I agree," he said. "This must have been done as a joke by someone with a warped sense of humour."

"I wonder," Jean thought.

Louise now discovered that back of the man with the shovel was a crudely carved arrow which pointed directly toward the scene. On a sudden hunch she asked the rancher, "In what direction of the compass does that arrow point?"

"Straight south," said Mr. Strong, "toward Lost Lake. I think your hunch about this newly made petroglyph representing the witch may be true."

Instantly Louise became worried. "Then the witch may be in danger!" she said. "This scene might have been chipped here as a message to someone who intends to harm her!"

Both Mr. Strong and Jean agreed, and Louise urged eagerly, "Let's leave at once and try to find out!"

The rancher shook his head. "I'd like to," he said, "but I must be home by six o'clock for an important appointment with a sheep buyer. It would be a fast, hard-riding two-day round trip to Lost Lake for a cowboy. But too rough for you girls to undertake in that time."

Seeing the disappointed looks on the Danas' faces, he added quickly, "I'll tell you what. If Baron isn't back by day after tomorrow, I'll take you to Lost Lake."

"That would be wonderful!" Jean exclaimed, smiling again.

Louise added her thanks, and with a twinkle in her eyes said that even if Baron did return, she still would like to take the ride and meet the witch of Lost Lake. "Leaving a mystery unsolved always bothers me," she added.

By this time the trio was hungry, and decided to eat lunch while the horses were resting and grazing on the sage grass. Jean was the first to finish, and she began exploring the gorge on foot.

Presently, from a distance, she called excitedly, "I've just found dog tracks!"

Eagerly Louise and Mr. Strong hurried forward. As they reached Jean's side, she said, "These prints certainly look like Baron's, but something about them seems different."

Mr. Strong examined the tracks, then said, "That's because the dog was running on three legs. He must have injured one paw."

"Poor Baron!" said Louise, but added hopefully, "This might mean he didn't go far beyond here. Now maybe we'll find him!"

She began calling his name but the dog did not respond.

"We'd better get the horses and make a search,"

Mr. Strong suggested. "No telling how far these tracks may lead."

The riders returned to their mounts and climbed into the saddles. It was not difficult to pick up the tracks of the limping dog.

Suddenly Mr. Strong, in the lead, reined up sharply. "Listen!" he exclaimed.

A short distance ahead they saw a box canyon. From it came the sounds of many dogs snarling and yapping. The Danas were horrified—had Baron become mixed up with a pack of wild dogs and gotten into a fight with them?

"Let's hurry!" Jean urged.

"We'd better ride up the slope and look down to see what's going on," the rancher advised. "Wild dogs sure shouldn't be met head on."

The Danas, extremely worried, obeyed and urged their mounts up the rocky bluff.

CHAPTER IV

Vanished Visitors

WHEN the riders reached a point on the incline from which they could look down into the box canyon, they saw a terrifying sight. Below them was a small pack of wild dogs, fighting ferociously. The din of their snarling was deafening.

"How horrible!" Louise exclaimed, as she looked from one dog to another, trying to spot Baron.

Jean, too, was gazing intently at the scene and presently was relieved not to find the beautiful German shepherd among the fighting dogs.

Mr. Strong said, "I guess the pack is battling to the death to choose a leader."

Jean sniffed and said, "If they don't stop pretty soon, there won't be anything left to lead!"

The rancher smiled. "There are no gentlemen animals in the wilds."

"Maybe not," said Louise, "but don't you think

we should try to stop the fight? Perhaps by throwing a rock down there to divert their attention?"

"It wouldn't do any good," Mr. Strong replied. "Let's go!"

As the riders brought their horses down the incline to the base of the gorge, Jean said the scene she had just witnessed made her still more frightened for Baron's safety.

"He may be with another pack of wild dogs, and when they come to choosing a leader, goodness only knows what will happen to him!"

Mr. Strong tried to reassure her. "You have no idea how well a dog as big and strong and intelligent as Baron can defend himself," he said.

"I suppose that's the way we should look at it," Louise replied with a sigh. "But we're forgetting about the witch. If Baron is at Lost Lake, he may be just as badly off as if he were with a pack of wild dogs!"

The rancher shrugged. "I can see that you're not going to be happy until you locate Baron—what's his full name?"

"Baron Otto von Neckar," Jean responded proudly. As she said the name she smiled.

Louise chuckled softly, adding, "It's quite a name for a dog, isn't it?"

"I'll say!" Mr. Strong remarked. "Our dog didn't do so well. Her name's just plain Eleanor, but she's very valuable, too—good sheep dog, good hunter, and a good guard at the ranch house."

The riders had just reached the floor of the gorge when a nondescript dog, running on three legs, hurried from the box canyon in their direction. For a moment the girls wondered if he might attack the horses, but instead he whined pitifully.

"I think he wants us to help him," said Louise.

"You don't suppose," Jean thought aloud, "that *he's* the dog whose tracks we found a little while ago."

"Most likely he is," Mr. Strong put in. "I guess it wasn't Baron after all."

Louise reined up and dismounted. At once the dog came to lick her hand.

"Why, you poor old fellow!" she said sympathetically. "You want us to fix your sore foot, don't you?"

To her amazement, the dog sat on his haunches and raised his right front paw.

"He must be somebody's pet!" Jean remarked, also getting off her horse.

"Or was, until recently," Mr. Strong observed. "He must have wandered off and now is a member of the pack, although he's not fully wild yet."

The sisters examined the animal's paw and quickly spotted a thorn.

"How can we ever pull it out?" Jean asked.

Louise grinned. "Believe it or not, I put a pair of

tweezers in my saddlebag. Ever since the time I rammed a thorn into my finger, I always carry a pair —just in case."

The dog proved to be gentle, and made no attempt to bite the girls as they "operated" on his paw. Finally, piece by piece, the thorn was extracted. Louise and Jean washed the wound in a trickling stream nearby and patted the paw dry with a paper handkerchief. The dog began to lick his paw vigorously, then stood up and jumped around. He wagged his tail furiously as if trying to offer his thanks.

"Now I suppose he'll go back to that wild pack," Louise surmised. "Too bad."

But she was wrong. As soon as Mr. Strong and the girls started off for the ranch, the animal followed them. By the time they arrived, he was completely exhausted and lay down outside the house.

When Mrs. Strong heard the story, she offered to take care of him and went for a bowl of meat. The dog ate the food quickly and flopped down once more. Soon afterward he got up, barked gratefully, and trotted away.

Mrs. Strong saw the dog leave. "I guess he didn't like my cooking," she said, shaking her head sadly.

"Oh, sure he did, Martha," her husband said cheerfully. "The little fellow just figured it was time to be joining his new friends again."

Louise and Jean took Rondy and Ginger into the barn stalls and rubbed them down. Then the girls gave the horses oats and water. Mr. Strong, after tending to Silver Streak, went to examine Jubilee's leg. He reported it much better and assured Jean she would be able to ride her the day after tomorrow. Then he went to talk to the sheep buyer who had arrived.

Mrs. Strong and Aunt Harriet had prepared a delicious dinner, which was served at seven o'clock. It included meat loaf with tomato gravy. One serving apiece was all the two women could eat, but Louise and Jean had seconds, and Mr. Strong managed to finish a third!

"I'm glad you liked it," Mrs. Strong said, "but I hope you saved room for my pumpkin pie!"

Jean, who adored pumpkin pie, grinned until her eyes were only slits. Then she sighed. "Oh, dear, I've eaten so much already. I don't know how I'll ever find room for dessert, but I'm certainly going to try!" She ate a piece.

Mr. Strong had said nothing, but a little later, almost sheepishly, he asked for a second serving! "Our pure fresh air gives one an appetite," he said by way of an excuse.

"I'm convinced of that!" Louise said, her eyes twinkling.

During the meal and for some time afterward the group discussed the witch, Lost Lake, and the missing Baron. Suddenly they heard Eleanor barking.

"She's probably scented some wild animal, and will chase after it," Mr. Strong said.

Instead, however, Eleanor barked more loudly than ever just outside the door. The rancher arose and opened it. In the late dusk he saw two men coming toward him. He stepped outside and called, "Halloo, there!"

"Hello!" they replied and one man added, "We're lost."

"Where are you from?" the rancher asked.

"The wrecked train."

Instantly the Dana girls were on their feet. "Passengers!" Jean exclaimed. "Maybe we'll recognize them."

"I wonder why they left the train," Louise mused.

By this time the two strangers had reached the ranch house and stepped into the living room. Neither of them looked familiar to the Danas.

"I'm Ben Hopley," said one, who was blond, short, and stocky. "This is my friend, Chet Simpson," he added.

Both men were about forty years old. Simpson was of medium height, had red hair, and eyes which the Dana girls thought were rather shifty.

"We came from the train too," Jean spoke up. "I thought it was supposed to pull out yesterday."

Chet Simpson said mournfully, "We got tired of hanging around and thought we'd take a walk. To tell you the truth, we got lost and spent the night in the woods. We've been walking ever since. Yours is the first ranch house we've seen. Will you direct us to the nearest station?"

"I suppose I could drive you there but not until tomorrow," Mr. Strong said.

Aunt Harriet spoke up. "If you're doing that and we find our lost dog before then, Louise and Jean and I could go with you."

"Lost dog?" Ben Hopley asked.

Baron's disappearance was explained to the men. Louise and Jean thought it strange that these travellers had not already heard the story—they thought everyone on the train knew about it by now.

"Have you men had supper?" Mrs. Strong asked.

"No, we haven't," Simpson replied.

At once Mrs. Strong offered to fix them a bite. Hopley smiled at her. "We'd like to ask an even bigger favour. Could you possibly rent us a room for the night?"

Mrs. Strong looked at her husband, who answered the question for her. "I'm afraid not, men. As a matter of fact, we haven't any more bedrooms than those which are being used."

Seeing the strangers' disappointed frowns, he added generously, "I'll tell you what I'll do, though. If you don't mind sleeping in the bunkhouse with my sheepherders, you can have a couple of empty cots out there."

"Oh, that would be perfectly all right," said Simpson. "Thanks."

As Hopley and Simpson ate the supper which Mrs. Strong had prepared for them, the men explained that they lived in New York and were in the wholesale clothing business.

"Where do you figure the missing dog went?" Hopley asked presently.

"We have no idea," Louise answered, but Mrs. Strong put in, "About thirty or forty miles from here there's a place called Lost Lake. A strange old woman lives there. Everybody calls her 'the witch.' We kind of think she may have the dog. Anyway, these girls want to go there and find out."

Hopley and Simpson looked at each other, startled, and asked for more details about the witch. They were told all that the Strongs knew about her.

"Queer story," Hopley commented. "Well," he said, arising from his chair, "I think, if you don't mind, I'll turn in. I'm not used to walking so far and I'm tired."

Both men said good night and Mr. Strong accompanied them to the bunkhouse. The others went to bed soon afterward and slept soundly.

Louise and Jean were awake early the next morning and decided to take a walk before breakfast. They had just stepped outside when they saw a small man, who wore a mustache and a large sombrero, racing excitedly toward the house.

At that moment Mr. Strong came outdoors. He said good morning to the Danas, then added, "Here comes my Mexican foreman, Juan Desido. Say, he looks worried! Wonder what's on his mind?"

The foreman rushed up, pulled off his hat, and said frantically, "Señor Strong, those two men you bring to bunkhouse last night! They have vanished!"

Mr. Strong smiled. "They're probably taking a walk."

"No! No! They leave before daylight. Gone when I wake up. Take three horses! Lot of food! Not go toward railroad, though. Go south!"

CHAPTER V

The Bunkhouse Clue

WHEN MR. STRONG heard his foreman's news of the stolen horses, he became red with anger. "So Hopley and Simpson are horse thieves and maybe something worse!" he cried bitterly. "To think that I was taken in by their silly story!"

Louise and Jean agreed that the two men were suave talkers. The girls, too, had thought Hopley and Simpson were telling the truth, but evidently the men had concocted the whole yarn just to steal the horses.

"They probably never even saw the train," Louise figured.

Juan Desido's face was dark with rage. "They're *diablos!*" he shouted. "Where those men go? Why?"

Mr. Strong did not reply. Instead, the rancher declared he would notify the sheriff by telephone of the theft. "Unless those two crooks hole up somewhere for a long time, I'm sure the sheriff or his deputies will find them pronto, especially if they don't know this territory well. They didn't talk like Westerners."

"Don't you think we should try hunting for them too?" Louise suggested.

The rancher smiled at the eager girl. "It might be dangerous," he said. "And, anyway, I couldn't go right away. I'm afraid I'll have to leave the investigating and capture to the sheriff."

Juan Desido, as well as the Dana girls, felt thwarted. All of them wanted to ride out at once and follow the prints left by the stolen horses. Reluctantly the three turned away, Juan to attend to his ranch duties and the girls to go into the house and assist with breakfast.

Aunt Harriet and Mrs. Strong were amazed and greatly disturbed to hear about Hopley and Simpson. The rancher's wife remarked, "I've always said, 'When you break bread with a stranger, watch your pocketbook!'"

The Danas laughed but admitted that they had indeed learned a lesson on caution from Hopley and Simpson.

Jean had a sudden thought. "Maybe," she said, "those men mean to try finding Baron themselves. They know he's valuable and could be sold for a good price."

"Oh, please don't say such things!" Miss Dana pleaded. "This situation is bad enough without adding *that* possibility."

An hour later three sheriff's deputies rode in. One of them explained that they had been nearby and the sheriff had contacted them by radio. The men were shown where the tracks of the stolen horses started. The posse set off at once and soon was out of sight. The Danas and Strongs watched them go, hoping their mission would be successful.

The thought of the men's adventure made the sisters restless. They longed to do something more exciting than just helping to feed the ranch animals!

"I have an idea!" Louise exclaimed. "Jean, why don't you and I look around *here* for clues to those thieves? It's possible they weren't using their right names. They might even be suspects wanted by the authorities!"

"That's a great idea," Jean agreed. "Where shall we start?"

"How about in the living room, then out in the direction from which the men came? After that, let's try the bunkhouse," Louise suggested.

The two young sleuths began their hunt. They came across nothing in the main room of the ranch house or on the grounds some distance from it. Seeing Mr. Strong in the paddock, the sisters went to talk to him. They explained their plan and asked if he would go with them to the bunkhouse.

"Certainly," he replied. "Anything to help find those crooks!"

He led the way to the bunkhouse and called in,

"Anybody here?" When there was no answer, Mr. Strong asked the girls, "Will you please wait a minute until I go inside?" With a grin he explained, "My sheepherders don't always tidy up the place to make it fit for visitors!"

In a few moments the rancher returned. "All clear," he announced, motioning the girls to enter. The sisters looked at each other in amusement. The place was immaculate, and surely Mr. Strong had not had time to do much straightening up himself. They imagined Juan Desido was a strict boss and a good housekeeper!

"Which bunks did Hopley and Simpson use?" Louise asked.

Mr. Strong pointed them out, and Louise began to check around one.

Jean took the other. Presently she called out, "Here's a tool under Hopley's bunk. Does this belong to the ranch?"

Mr. Strong walked over and took the battered implement from her. "Why, this is a tool for chipping stone," he said. "It's damaged and doesn't belong to the ranch."

"Then it must belong to one of the horse thieves!" Jean cried exultantly. "Probably Ben Hopley, since it was under his bunk."

Louise had been thinking fast. Her mind immediately recalled the newly made petroglyph the girls had discovered in the cave and the piece of **tool they had found there.**

Seeing the excited look on her sister's face, Jean said, "I know what you're thinking, Louise—that Ben Hopley might have chipped out that picture of the witch with the man behind her holding the shovel and ready to strike."

"That's right," Louise admitted. "Maybe Hopley and Simpson are the ones who intend to harm the witch!"

Mr. Strong was intrigued with the girls' reasoning. "Do you suppose those men know the secret of Lost Lake?" he asked. "And pretended to be surprised at the witch story?"

"But what *is* the secret?" Jean asked.

"That's a good question," the rancher replied. "Personally, I have always thought that the witch must be staying there for some other reason than just digging up enough artifacts to buy food, clothing, and a new horse now and then."

"You mean she's digging for something really valuable, and Hopley and Simpson know this?" Louise asked worriedly.

"That's my guess," the rancher answered.

The Danas wished they might set out at once for Lost Lake. Now they had three incentives: to find Baron, to warn the witch, and possibly to locate the thieves and retrieve the stolen horses. But they had to be content to wait until the following day when the rancher could accompany them.

"We should start at sunrise," said Mr. Strong. "And pack some warm clothes," the rancher added.

"Old codgers around here forecast an open winter, but you never know!"

The girls were up before dawn. They dressed quickly and were astride their mounts when the rancher was ready to leave. This time the trio was taking a pack horse to carry their food, sleeping bags, and extra sweaters.

The sheriff had phoned, reporting the posse had had no success. Aunt Harriet wished the searchers luck, and the three set off at a good clip. Presently they left the flat land behind.

Mr. Strong chose a trail which finally led through various canyons. The Danas were intrigued by the fantastic rock formations, with their riot of colour. Overhanging cliffs looked like birds' heads, and the rock walls of pinkish red, tan, brown, blue, and purple made an unbelievable and beautiful picture.

Mr. Strong rested the horses every few miles. At ten o'clock he called a longer halt.

"I don't know about you girls," he said, grinning, "but I'm starved!"

Jean said as she dismounted, "One of those great big ham-cheese-and-tomato sandwiches would sure taste good to me!"

After the sandwiches, there were oranges and homemade biscuits. When the trio finished eating, Louise took out a camera from her saddlebag, and after she and Jean had snapped a few pictures, the riders set off once more.

The horses walked slowly now. The going through the next canyon was very rough and a stiff wind had come up. In a short while snow began to fall. Mr. Strong suggested that they stop in a cave a short distance ahead. By the time they reached it, the girls were glad to take advantage of the shelter. The snow was being whipped about by the high wind and the sisters' faces stung.

"This is just a squall," Mr. Strong assured them.

The horses were taken inside the cave, which was a large one, and according to Mr. Strong had been used as a home by Indians long ago. There were no petroglyphs or pictographs on the walls which were black, probably from the smoke of cooking fires.

"How long do you think this snowstorm will last?" Louise asked Mr. Strong, as she peered out at what looked like a white hurricane.

"Oh, half an hour perhaps," he answered, and showed no alarm. "This won't snow us in."

The travellers sat down on the earthen floor. Idly the Danas began to poke their fingers into the dry earth.

"Wouldn't it be fun to find an artifact?" Louise remarked.

"There ought to be some old things buried here," said Mr. Strong. "I have a small trowel in my saddlebag. I'll get it and you can try your luck."

He went for the tool and handed it to Jean, who began digging furiously. She found nothing.

But Louise, who had been kicking up the dirt with the heel of her boot a little distance away, said, "Here's an arrowhead."

She showed the ancient object to the others, then put it into her pocket.

Jean had continued digging. Suddenly she cried out excitedly, "I've found something big! It looks as if it might be valuable!"

CHAPTER VI

A Mysterious Light

Louise hurried across the cave and peered into the hole which Jean had dug. It was fairly wide and rather deep. At the bottom could be seen a worn buckskin pouch. Gently Jean scooped up the ancient bag which was tied round and round at the top with a leather thong.

"I wonder what's inside!" she said excitedly, laying the pouch on the ground. Carefully she opened it.

"Feathers!" chorused the sisters.

As Jean lifted out the whole piece, they saw that the feathers were part of an ornate Indian head-dress.

"It's beautiful!" Louise observed.

The headband was made from hundreds of black and orange flicker feathers. Below them was a circle of trimming which looked like ermine.

"That's right nice," Mr. Strong commented admiringly. "Jean, you've made a real find."

"What kind of animal did this fur come from?" Jean asked, pleased at his praise.

"Winter weasels," the rancher replied, then explained he meant that in winter, weasels take on this white colouring and the tips of their tails become black. "Then we call them ermines. Winter's the season when the fur and skins are best."

Jean set the headdress on her hair and began to dance around with stately steps. "Do I look like an Indian princess?" she asked, grinning.

"Not with that undignified smile," her sister teased.

Mr. Strong looked closely at the headdress and remarked that the ancient Indians of California had also used unusually beautiful ceremonial headdresses made of birds' feathers. "There may be some connection between the Indians who lived there and the tribes around here," he said thoughtfully.

"And even a connection with the old Polynesians that lived in the Hawaiian Islands," Louise said. "In a museum in Honolulu, Jean and I saw a whole cape and warrior's headpiece made of feathers. Do you suppose ancient Polynesian explorers came all the way to this country?"

Mr. Strong shrugged. "Our historians and archaeologists still have a great deal to learn about the migrations of various peoples on this earth."

Louise had picked up the trowel and now decided to try her luck. "Maybe I can make a discovery here too!"

She dug around the edges of the hole and scooped out a good-sized pile of dirt without finding anything. At last, however, she was rewarded and held up a pair of deerskin moccasins. Louise pulled off her boots and tried to put them on. They were much too small!

"Hm," she said in mock disgust. "White girl have big feet. Indian man have dainty feet!"

The others burst out laughing.

Jean carefully folded up her prize headdress, put it back into the buckskin pouch, and placed this in her saddlebag. Louise tucked the moccasins into hers.

"I suppose we should give these pieces to a museum," Louise remarked.

"Yes, you really should," Mr. Strong agreed. "Any ancient, rare find should be put into a safe, permanent exhibit under glass away from the air. Then people can enjoy it without fear of its being damaged."

By this time the roaring gale had greatly diminished and the snowstorm had ceased. Mr. Strong and the Danas led their horses from the cave and climbed into the saddles.

Suddenly they heard a loud whinny. It was not from one of their mounts!

"Somebody else is in this canyon!" Jean cried out.

At that very moment Louise, who was in the lead, saw two men on horseback emerge from an under-cut cliff some distance beyond. One, whose face she could not see, rode off quickly. The other was having trouble with his horse which was dancing around as if it did not want to go forward.

The rider was Ben Hopley!

Quickly Louise relayed this information to her companions and the three urged their horses into a gallop. The riders ahead had evidently spotted them, and did the same.

There was a sharp turn in the canyon, and within a few seconds the men were out of sight. When Mr. Strong and the girls reached the turn, the fugitives had disappeared. The pursuers looked up each of the canyon walls. They noted that the walls were not steep, and a horse could have negotiated them without danger. But there was no sign of the horses or the men.

"Is there a cave nearby where they could be hiding?" Louise asked, seeing prints ahead.

"Not that I know of," Mr. Strong answered. The rancher looked worried, nevertheless.

He and the Danas continued on. The canyon floor widened, with sagebrush and a variety of native ground-cover herbage, including dry filaree, growing profusely on it. This acted as a cushion for the horses' feet, so the three riders continued to move ahead at full speed.

The canyon ended abruptly. Beyond stretched

an open expanse. But Hopley and his pal were not in sight.

"Where could those men have gone?" Jean asked in disgust.

"It beats me," said Mr. Strong. "But one thing I'm sure of—Hopley and Simpson are not new to this area, even though they said they're from New York. A person unfamiliar with this territory couldn't possibly have disappeared this easily."

"We haven't seen any more horseshoe prints," said Louise, looking over the ground carefully.

Mr. Strong pointed to a stream. It appeared to be slightly muddy, as if recently disturbed by a moving object. "We lost the trail of those riders because they took their horses through the water," he said.

"Well, I'm certain we're in no danger," Mr. Strong added. "Those men are after something, but I don't think they'll risk coming out in the open to harm us in order to accomplish it."

Jean asked him if the route the rancher was taking led directly to Lost Lake.

"That depends on which end of the lake you want to hit," he replied, "the water that remains, or the far side where the mountain tumbled into it."

The young sleuth laughed. "I thought I might have a clue to which way Hopley and Simpson went," she said. "But they could have taken either way toward Lost Lake. So I think we should go to the section you think the witch lives in."

"I'm not sure of that myself," the rancher said. "But, according to hearsay, her place is not far from the water."

Louise had been gazing around as an idea came to her. Now she remarked, "My guess is that Hopley and Simpson aren't sure where the witch is, either. When they saw us, they probably figured *we* know and they've doubled back so they can follow us."

"Well," said Mr. Strong, "you're a better detective than I am. I hadn't thought of that. We'd better be mighty careful," he warned. "You girls ride ahead. I'll bring up the rear and keep turning around to see if I can catch a glimpse of 'em."

The riders went on, and whenever Mr. Strong wanted to change directions, he called out instructions to Louise, who was leading the way.

By four o'clock the group was hungry again and stopped to rest and eat supper. Mr. Strong informed the Danas he was trying to reach a deserted cabin some miles ahead.

"We'll spend the night there," he said. "I'd prefer that you girls be under cover if possible."

He told them that he had discovered the cabin while he was on a hunting trip some time ago.

"It's very old—dates back to around 1880, but it has stood up remarkably well. It's quite crude of course—built of cottonwood, cedar, and piñon logs. The roof is made of dirt and willow and cedar bark. The floor's dirt, too," he added. "Do you girls mind sleeping on the ground?"

"We've done it many times when camping out," Jean assured him.

"Good! I thought maybe you girls were only used to fancy hotels and stuff like that." The rancher laughed. "This log cabin I'm taking you to doesn't have any windows—just chinks between the logs for air and light! I guess for safety too!"

"It must be kind of chilly in the wintertime," Louise remarked.

"Oh, there's a great big fireplace," Mr. Strong told her. "A good roaring fire in it will take care of us!"

The riders started off once more. Mr. Strong said that whenever the terrain made it feasible for the horses to canter, they should be urged to do this.

"The sun goes down all of a sudden in these mountains," he explained. "It might be very difficult to find the cabin if we don't get there before dark."

Just then the group came to a dead-end canyon. Mr. Strong berated himself for making the wrong turn. He directed that they pull around and go back to where there was a branching trail which led through a gorge. Louise and Jean knew from the rancher's silence the past fifteen minutes that he was concerned about their reaching the cabin, with its protection from wild animals, before dark.

After a while, however, he announced cheerily, "We're on the right trail! The cabin's only about a mile away."

Jean was now in the lead and it was not long before she spotted the rustic building a short distance away. At the same moment the sun sank below the horizon.

Jean gave a start, then exclaimed, "Someone's in the cabin! I can see light coming through the chinks!"

Louise saw the light too and said worriedly, "The horse thieves—Hopley and Simpson!"

CHAPTER VII

On Watch

THERE were mixed emotions among the three riders. All felt elated that perhaps they had found the thieves and would get back the stolen horses. They also knew that any attempt at capture might be dangerous—Hopley and Simpson probably had guns!

There was the possibility, too, the Danas realized, that the occupants of the cabin were *not* the men they sought.

Louise spoke up. "If the people in the cabin *are* the thieves, your stolen horses must be tethered nearby, Mr. Strong. Would you know your own animals?"

"I think so," the rancher replied with a grin. "In any case, they'd know me!"

"Then why don't we hunt for the horses?" Louise went on. "If we find them, we can decide what to do next."

"A good idea," Mr. Strong agreed.

Jean had another suggestion. "Couldn't we hide the horses so the men can't escape, and then ride off and notify the sheriff?"

The rancher shook his head. "I'm afraid that would take too long. By the time we could get word to the sheriff, the thieves probably would have run away. And finding anyone in these canyons is a real task. Criminals have been known to hide out here for years."

Mr. Strong said, however, that he was certainly in favour of their sneaking up to look for any horses. It was not easy to make a search because of the darkness and the rough terrain. Progress was slow, but finally the trio succeeded in making a complete circle of the cabin. There were no horses near it.

"That's very strange," Mr. Strong remarked. "Nobody could reach this place except on a horse."

Jean urged that they walk directly up to the cabin and knock on the door.

Louise at once vetoed this idea. "We might become prisoners!" she protested. "Why don't we sneak up closer and just listen? We may get some evidence."

Mr. Strong approved of this suggestion and the three went forward on tiptoe. As they neared the cabin, a woman's voice became audible.

"Pretty crude cookin' utensils here," she said.

A man's voice answered, "You're lucky to have what's on hand."

"How long do you think we'll be in this horrible place?" the woman asked in a nasal whine.

"Ask me something easy," the man replied. "Just be glad you're here with your husband instead of alone, with some wild animals prowling around!"

The Danas and Mr. Strong exchanged glances. The couple inside definitely were not the horse thieves.

The trio listened for a while longer to be sure the occupants of the cabin would not be unfriendly if approached. From the conversation that ensued between the husband and wife, the listeners judged that the couple were rather common people and were from the East.

"They sound okay," Mr. Strong whispered finnally. "I guess it's safe to make our presence known. We'll walk off a distance and announce ourselves."

The three went about a hundred feet from the cabin, then Mr. Strong called out in a loud voice, "Halloo, there!"

Almost at once the door opened and a large man about thirty-five years old called back, "Who's there?"

"Riders from the Strong ranch," the ranchman replied as he and the two girls stepped forward quickly.

By this time the stranger's wife had appeared in the doorway. She, too, was about thirty-five years old, wore very tight-fitting riding clothes, and had artificial-looking blond hair, piled high on her head, which stuck out in wisps over her forehead and neck.

"We're Mr. and Mrs. Sam Rinehart," the man introduced himself and his wife. "What can we do for you?"

The rancher explained that he and the girls were on a riding trip and had planned to make an overnight stop at the cabin, which he thought was empty. "You're living here?" he asked.

"Not any longer than we have to," Mrs. Rinehart spoke up in an irritated tone.

"Well, come in," her husband invited, but the riders felt there was little warmth in the suggestion.

Louise and Jean stepped inside. Mr. Strong followed. The one room of the building was fairly large and pleasant, but at the moment very untidy. Empty and unrinsed food cans stood on a tiny, old-fashioned sink. Two tin cups and battered plates, showing evidence of a recent meal, were on a small table at one side of the room.

"This is wild country!" said Mr. Rinehart. "Sally and I were with a group of people. We were buck hunting but got separated from the others."

"And found your way here—on foot?" Mr. Strong inquired, amazed.

"You bet. We got chased, didn't we, Sam?" Mrs. Rinehart said. "By a big bear!"

"Yeah," her husband answered. "Ferocious

beast. Almost clawed us. We just made this place in time."

"That's right," said Sally Rinehart. "Oh, it was something awful. Now we're afraid to go out. We hope by morning some of the other hunters will come for us."

"Did you find this cabin stocked with food and these kerosene lanterns?" Mr. Strong asked.

"Yes. Pretty fortunate, eh?" said Sam Rinehart. "Want something to eat?"

"Thanks," replied Mr. Strong, "but we have plenty of provisions on our pack horse. I'll go get some for supper."

"I'll go with you," Sam Rinehart offered, and the two men left the cabin.

Sally Rinehart turned to the Danas and gave a huge sigh. "When our friends find us," she said, "I sure hope they bring our horses. I'm so tired of walking I could die."

"I can imagine," Louise murmured politely.

The woman did not offer to clear the table, and sank into a chair. Louise carried the dirty dishes to the sink while Jean wiped the table. By this time the men had returned. The food they brought—cans of meat, biscuits, and fruit—was laid on the table.

As the trio from the Strong ranch ate, Jean asked the Rineharts if they had seen a police dog wandering around. "One which belongs to us disappeared," she said, but evaded telling the whole story.

The Rineharts looked at each other, then Sam answered, "No, we didn't see any police dog. Sorry you lost yours. But while we were hunting we met a couple of men who told us a story about a valuable police dog."

"What was it?" Louise asked quickly.

"They said there had been a train wreck north of here. Right afterward, a police dog ran away from his owner. It seems the dog was gone for several hours, but just before the train pulled out, he came back. Terrific how those animals pick up a scent, don't you think?"

"Yes, it is," Mr. Strong agreed.

Louise and Jean said nothing. Was the dog Mr. Rinehart mentioned really Baron? Had the sisters come on a wild-goose chase? And if the dog *was* back on the train, why hadn't the conductor notified the Strongs?

"When Baron didn't find us, he may have run away again," Jean thought worriedly.

She and Louise felt, however, that Mr. Strong was wary of the Rineharts and their story. For this reason, they did not divulge the fact that they had been on the same train. Instead, the girls changed the subject.

"Mr. and Mrs. Rinehart," said Jean, "while you were deer hunting, did you see the witch of Lost Lake?"

At this, Sam Rinehart burst into laughter. "The witch? No, we didn't see her because the old woman's gone."

"Gone!" cried the Danas and Mr. Strong.

"That's right. We heard back in town that she must have died or moved away. Anyhow, her cabin is deserted, according to the storekeeper who told us the story."

The sisters and the rancher made no comment. The Danas felt very much let down. It seemed as if their trek to Lost Lake with Mr. Strong was proving to be a miserable failure.

The girls gathered up the food wrappings and cans left from their supper, then everyone decided to go to bed. There were two cots in the cabin, which Jean insisted her sister and Mrs. Rinehart use.

"I'll have more room on the floor!" she said, chuckling, and crawled into her sleeping bag. Mr. Strong and Sam Rinehart took theirs outside.

Louise and Jean could not sleep. They lay in the darkness recalling all the events of the day, and puzzling over the mysteries of Baron and the witch. Presently bright moonlight began to show through the chinks of the cabin wall.

Around midnight the Danas saw Sally Rinehart, slowly and noiselessly, rise from her cot and go toward the door. As she opened it, the girls caught a glimpse of Sam Rinehart standing outside. The next instant the couple disappeared from sight.

"Jean, are you awake?" Louise asked softly.

"Yes."

"I believe," Louise said, "that the Rineharts are phonies and are going to steal our horses!"

"Then we must get Mr. Strong and stop them!" Jean cried. "Come on!"

The girls dashed from the cabin. At that very second a shot rang out!

CHAPTER VIII

Eerie Echoes

In the moonlight Louise and Jean could see Sam and Sally Rinehart riding away on two horses.

"Silver Streak and Jubilee!" Louise gasped.

Mr. Strong had given chase after the couple and was firing into the air, apparently hoping to discourage their escape.

"We'd better not try it, Sam!" the Danas heard Sally Rinehart call out to her husband.

"Go on!" he ordered angrily.

"But I don't want to be shot!" she wailed.

In desperation, Sam leaped from his horse and mounted Jubilee behind his wife. He slapped the mare hard on the rump and she galloped off.

Mr. Strong continued running until he reached Silver Streak, who had slowed to a walk. The rancher started to mount, then changed his mind. He waited until the girls caught up to him.

"Aren't you going after them?" Jean asked, surprised. "They're thieves!"

Mr. Strong explained that he did not want to leave the Danas alone. "After what has happened, I'm afraid it isn't very safe around here. Something queer is going on."

"But I hate to lose Jubilee," Jean said sorrowfully.

Louise looked intently at Mr. Strong. "You suspected that couple all along, didn't you? Why?"

"Because their story was too thin," the rancher answered. "If they're both hunters, why didn't one of them shoot the bear they claimed was after them?"

"Yes, why not?" Louise repeated.

"And why," Mr. Strong went on, "if the Rineharts had horses of their own, didn't they go back and get them? They're phonies, all right."

Louise then speculated as to whether the couple had really found the food in the cabin. "Or had they brought it with the intention of staying there? And did our arrival interfere with some plan the Rineharts were carrying out?"

"I think you're right," the rancher agreed.

"Who can they be, and what were they planning?" Jean inquired. "Maybe they're using false names!"

"Yes," said Louise. "And I don't believe the Rineharts' story about Baron going back to the train."

"Neither do I," Jean agreed. "But maybe they did hear it, and I'll bet if they did, the story came from Hopley and Simpson whom they must have met."

"But why would those men tell such a thing?" Mr. Strong asked.

"They hoped we'd meet the Rineharts, hear about Baron, and hurry away from here," Jean declared. "Hopley and Simpson just don't want us around this area!"

"You might be right," the rancher said thoughtfully.

Despite the gravity of the situation, Mr. Strong smiled as they walked back to the cabin. "I hope you girls won't carry away a bad opinion of our big, beautiful Rocky Mountain country."

"Not at all," said Jean, grinning back. "No matter where you go you find thieves around!"

"And *these* thieves were imported, don't forget!" Louise added.

The rancher became serious again. "Without the extra horse, we'll have to give up our trip to Lost Lake," he said. "We must start back at dawn. Anyway, I want to report to the sheriff everything that has happened."

"And I want to check the Rineharts' version of the dog story," said Jean.

The two girls dozed fitfully for the next few hours, but Mr. Strong remained on guard. Nothing unusual occurred. After a hasty breakfast and tidying up the cabin, the three riders set off. Jean insisted upon taking the pack horse, on whom extra blankets were laid.

"Riding bareback in the Rockies!" she called gaily. "I feel like an Indian!"

It was arranged that Jean would go in the lead, with the others close by in case of trouble. But she rode very well.

About midmorning Louise exclaimed admiringly about the beautiful scene ahead. A sheer rock wall arose on the left of the flat land, while some distance to the right was a low hill of stunted pines.

"What an unusual sight!" Jean remarked.

The riders did not talk for a few minutes as they took in the gorgeous panorama. Suddenly they were startled by a clear, well-defined voice calling:

"Get the witch! Get the witch! Get the witch!"

The three on horseback reined up abruptly. There was absolute silence. The mysterious voice said no more.

Finally Mr. Strong spoke up in a whisper, "It's an echo from the wall. Don't talk—let's try to find the person who caused the echo."

The girls strained their eyes to look among the trees opposite the wall. They could see no movement. Quickly they galloped across the flat land and again scanned the hillside. No one was revealed, although it would have been almost impossible for a person to hide among the stunted pines.

"This place sure is spooky," Jean whispered as they rode on.

"And what was meant by the caller?" Louise asked.

When the mystified riders reached the end of the rock wall and were about to turn sharply around the base of it, they were startled to hear laughter—not lilting, happy laughter, but the type which is characteristic of a person with a sardonic nature.

The laughter was followed by the words, "Beautiful artwork! Beautiful artwork! Beautiful artwork!"

The riders reined up again and looked in every direction. Still they could see no one.

"What do you make of it?" Louise finally asked Mr. Strong in a low voice.

The rancher shook his head in puzzlement. "I can't figure it out. All I can tell you is I understand there's a certain rock wall in this area which repeats words in a triple echo. This must be that wall."

"I'd certainly like to know who's causing the echo," Jean stated.

"We may as well go on," Mr. Strong urged. "This incident is just one more circumstance to report to the sheriff."

The Danas would have liked to search the area more thoroughly, but they followed their host's advice and went on. Nevertheless, the trio continued to discuss the weird words they had heard.

"What in the world could they mean?" Jean asked. "They just don't seem to make sense."

"It's my guess," said Mr. Strong, "that the person saying those things was pulling a stunt, or is plain mad."

"That may be part of the mystery of Lost Lake," Louise suggested.

"Could be," the rancher agreed. "Well, I suppose one of these days the whole thing will be solved."

As soon as they reached the ranch, the girls asked Aunt Harriet if any message had come about Baron. The answer was no. Mr. Strong then telephoned the sheriff about having seen Hopley and Simpson, the Rineharts, and the stolen horse, Jubilee.

"By the way, Sheriff," he added, "would you mind contacting the railroad station at Green River and finding out whether the valuable German shepherd dog that ran away from the wreck returned and went aboard?"

Louise and Jean had heard the question and now stood nearby awaiting the answer. As they all listened, the sheriff's voice came loud and clear.

"That story about a German shepherd dog was not true. None ever came to the train."

CHAPTER IX

The Explosion

THE sheriff's report deepened the Danas' concern for Baron. It seemed certain now that the dog was still somewhere in the Rocky Mountains, a possible prey for wild beasts. The girls wondered again whether the Rineharts had concocted the train story.

"I'm convinced they aren't above telling such a lie for some underhand reason," Louise surmised.

"Do you think they weren't telling the truth about the witch, either?" her sister asked.

"I'll bet they weren't," Louise answered. "I'd certainly like to verify their story that the witch is either dead or has moved away."

Before the girls had a chance to discuss the matter further, Aunt Harriet asked them to go for a short walk with her. They left the ranch house and set off across a grazing field.

Presently Miss Dana smiled and said, "I didn't

ask you girls to come with me just for the exercise. I wanted to tell you that I think we have imposed on the Strongs long enough."

Louise and Jean made no comment. Both realized Aunt Harriet's statement was true, yet they hated the thought of leaving the area without having retrieved Baron and possibly solving the secret of Lost Lake.

Their aunt read the girls' minds. "I know you're eager to continue your sleuthing, and I must admit I get a chill every time I think of having to notify Baron's new and old owners about what has happened. Nevertheless, we have no assurance and no leads that the dog will be found."

"You're right, of course, Aunt Harriet," said Louise. "But couldn't we stay *one* more day? I'd like to follow a hunch I have."

"What's that?" her aunt asked.

"I'd like to go to town and question some of the people there as to what they know about the witch of Lost Lake. We may pick up a clue and might even find out that she's still at her cabin and has Baron."

"Yes," Jean added eagerly. "Or perhaps someone in town has seen Baron and could give us a new angle on which to work."

Miss Dana smiled. "Very well. You may have a day in town, then we must ask Mr. Strong to drive us to the Green River railroad station."

The three Danas turned back toward the ranch

house. As they approached it, Aunt Harriet chuckled. "How are we going to get to town?" she asked. "I don't plan to ride a horse all that way!"

The girls laughed, then Louise said, "I thought maybe we could borrow the Strongs' jeep."

When they went back to the ranch house, Mrs. Strong greeted them with a worried look. "You know," she said, "it's bad luck to leave a house and come back, then start right out again."

The Danas looked puzzled. The rancher's wife went on, "Oh, I can read your minds. You went outside to talk about leaving and you're going to start packing."

The three Danas burst into laughter. "You really are psychic," said Aunt Harriet. "The truth is, we think we've imposed on your kindness long enough and should be on our way home."

Mrs. Strong pursed her lips disapprovingly. "Nonsense," she said. "Outside of the fact that Louise and Jean want to solve the mystery, you can't go off and leave me in the middle of making that new hooked rug for my daughter."

Louise and Jean now learned that Aunt Harriet, who was an expert at rug hooking, had, during their absence, helped Mrs. Strong with a rather complicated pattern. The rug was to be an anniversary gift to her daughter and would have to be sent off in a few days in order to reach her in time for the occasion.

"Well—" Miss Dana began.

"No ifs, ands, or buts," Mrs. Strong said decisively. "You people are going to stay. I'll confess to you that it's really lonesome here when John's away. I've thoroughly enjoyed you folks, and I'd love to have you stay as long as you can."

She chuckled. "There's really no necessity of your getting home for a while yet, since the girls don't have to go back to school until after Thanksgiving."

Jean nodded. "And Uncle Ned won't be home till then."

Captain Dana, who commanded an ocean liner, was Aunt Harriet's brother. They lived in Oak Falls, and had reared Louise and Jean, children of their deceased brother and sister-in-law.

"What you say is true," Aunt Harriet replied, smiling. "As to the rug, I'll be very happy to help you finish it. But as soon as it's ready, we absolutely must go."

Jean chuckled. "That gives Louise and me a nice extension of time to find Baron and find out if any harm came to the witch. I can't get that petroglyph out of my mind," she said. "Louise, we'll really have to move fast, though!"

It was arranged that the next morning Mrs. Strong would drive Miss Dana and the girls to Rawhide, which she said was a typical small Rocky Mountain town with one general store.

"Caleb Winthrop, the proprietor, carries everything you can think of," she said. Chuckling, she added, "He not only sells yarn, which I need, but tells yarns!"

The others laughed and Jean said, "Then he probably knows all the local news. Maybe he can tell us whether or not the witch is still at Lost Lake."

"I'm sure he can," Mrs. Strong answered.

The sisters could hardly wait for morning to come.

Directly after breakfast they set off in the jeep. Mrs. Strong proved to be a careful driver which was fortunate, because the dirt lane from the ranch out to the main road leading to Rawhide was rough and uneven from the hoof marks of sheep crossing and recrossing it.

The trip to Rawhide took nearly two hours. The town was situated in an open area, but was surrounded by hills and bushy wasteland grey green with sage.

The general store proved to be a delight for the Danas. It was large, and had shelves and cases filled with everything one would need for housekeeping and the running of a ranch, except the animals! There was a complete hardware department, including farm machinery. The girls strolled over to look at the various implements.

As they rejoined the women at the notions counter, Jean said with a giggle, "This is a super-duper supermarket!"

Mrs. Strong introduced Louise and Jean to the

proprietor, who immediately told them he was an old-timer in these parts. "There ain't a thing goin' on within a hundred miles around here that I don't know about!" Mr. Winthrop boasted.

"Then you're just the man we want to talk to," said Louise. "We're very much interested in the stories about a witch living at Lost Lake. Do you know anything about her?"

Caleb Winthrop scratched his head. "You would ask me a hard one," he replied, his eyes twinkling. "Nobody knows much about her. I heard from a friend of mine up in Huntersville where she sometimes comes to shop that she still lives there."

"We heard she had either died or moved away," Jean spoke up.

"That's not so," Mr. Winthrop answered. "One of my boys was up to Huntersville day before yesterday. He saw her there with her horse, buyin' supplies."

The Danas felt that they had practically proved their point. The Rineharts' story about the witch had *not* been true!

"It's generally believed," Caleb Winthrop went on, "that the witch is guardin' some secret, but what it is nobody has ever found out. Of course there have been guesses."

"What are they?" Jean inquired quickly.

Mr. Winthrop said it was thought that possibly when the witch returned to the lake after the earthquake she had found some member of her family badly maimed and was protecting him from gossipy townsfolk.

"Maybe you'd like to read about the catastrophe," said the storekeeper. "I have a copy here of the Huntersville newspaper which came out right after the earthquake and landslide."

"We'd love to see it," Louise told him.

Mr. Winthrop went to his office at the rear. Presently he returned with the yellowed, fragile forty-year-old newspaper.

In reading about the disaster, the girls learned that originally the body of water now known as Lost Lake had been called Pueblo Lake.

According to the news items, no one had survived the landslide. There was a list of those who had lost their lives. Louise and Jean ran down the list.

On it were a Mr. and Mrs. Antonio Carmino and in another part of the paper Louise came across a small item, saying that the Carminos' twenty-year-old daughter, named Blanche, was out of town at the time of the disaster.

"She may be the person who's now called the witch!" Louise exclaimed.

"Could be," Caleb Winthrop admitted.

The girls read every page of the old newspaper but could find nothing which gave a clue to any present-day secret of Lost Lake.

Suddenly Louise asked, "How far is it to Huntersville, Mrs. Strong?"

"Oh, it's only fifty miles." Mrs. Strong chuckled. "I know you girls would like to go there, so why don't we?"

The Danas hugged her, saying, "You're a darling. You sure you don't mind?"

After making several purchases, including sandwiches, and yarn for the hooked rug, the ranchwoman was ready to leave. When they were seated in the jeep once more, she said, "I'm glad we've decided to visit Huntersville. I didn't think of it before, but there's a very interesting place on the way that you people ought to see. It's a mountain where a great many dinosaur bones have been dug up."

The girls were eager to see it, and when they finally came near the rocky, chaparral-dotted slope, Mrs. Strong pulled over and stopped.

"Would you girls like to do a little climbing?" she asked, and added jokingly, "Maybe you can see the backbone of one of those prehistoric reptiles."

Everyone alighted, and while the women watched, Louise and Jean hurried across a small, flat area at the foot of the ancient sandstone mountain. Then they began to climb. A few minutes later the girls paused for breath and scanned the slope in every direction.

"Nothing to look at here except stones and bushes," Jean remarked.

Louise was not so sure of this. "I see humpy

ridges over there." She pointed to their left. "Jean," she asked excitedly, "do you suppose they could be the backbone of a dinosaur fossil?"

"Let's find out!" Jean said eagerly.

Cautiously and arduously the two girls made their way to the spot. They had just reached it, and were starting to investigate the strange, lengthwise ridges when from the distance came a great *boom.*

"An explosion!" Louise exclaimed.

The words were hardly out of her mouth when the mountain seemed to give a convulsive shudder. The next moment a landslide started just above the girls. Within seconds, rocks and dirt came hurtling toward them.

There was no escape for Louise and Jean. They were knocked over and carried downward with the tumbling debris!

CHAPTER X

Prehistoric Discovery

"Oh!" cried Miss Harriet Dana, as she saw her nieces rolling down the mountainside amid the bouncing rocks, uprooted bushes, and flying dirt.

Mrs. Strong, too, was aghast at the sight. She hurried after Aunt Harriet toward the steep slope, dodging the stones which were flying in every direction.

By the time the women reached Louise and Jean, the girls were sitting up at the bottom of the hillside.

"Are you hurt?" the sisters were asking each other.

Both smiled ruefully. Louise and Jean had suffered no serious injuries, but were disheveled, dirty, and scratched and bruised. Aunt Harriet and Mrs. Strong knelt anxiously beside them until convinced that the girls really were unharmed.

"It's a miracle!" said Aunt Harriet. Then she added, "I wonder what caused the landslide."

Louise asked the two women if they had heard the loud boom just before the landslide had occurred. "There must have been an explosion and the vibration loosened the earth and rocks."

Mrs. Strong told them there was a quarry some distance away on the other side of the road. "No doubt the men are blasting," she said.

"We'd better get away from here before anything else happens," Miss Dana urged.

Suddenly Jean had an idea. "Do you suppose any dinosaur bones were uncovered by the landslide?" she asked, then explained how Louise had detected certain humps which she thought indicated a dinosaur's backbone. "Please, let's take a look before we leave."

"What do you think?" Aunt Harriet asked Mrs. Strong. "You know more about this territory than we do."

"There is usually a long interval between the blasts at the quarry," the ranchwoman answered. "I think it's safe to stay down here, but I don't know about climbing up this mountain again to look for a fossil."

The girls, however, persuaded their aunt that they did not want to miss this opportunity of, perhaps, making a great discovery.

"You win!" Miss Dana smiled. "I'll even come along."

"And I," Mrs. Strong said.

All four began to climb. They found the going difficult as there was still a quantity of loose rocks and dirt on the slope.

Louise was the first to reach the spot where the girls had detected the humps before the landslide had occurred. She cried out excitedly, "Yes! Here are some bones!"

As the rest came up and examined her find, they could plainly make out part of the backbone of a dinosaur!

Louise was overjoyed. "This is about the most exciting thing that's ever happened in my life!" she exclaimed.

Jean grinned. "Your name will go down with the great," she teased.

"We must report this wonderful find immediately to our Department of Natural Resources," said Mrs. Strong. "If you girls feel up to it, we'll go on to Huntersville and stop at Deputy Sheriff Alt's office."

Louise and Jean declared they felt perfectly all right. "But we're an absolute mess!" Jean wailed.

Martha Strong chuckled. "I carry a complete clean-up kit in the jeep. I never know when I might have to change a tire or work on the engine and I hate looking dirty."

When they reached the car, she brought out a large plastic bag containing cold cream, paper handkerchiefs, and towels. She also produced a large jug of water and a nail brush. In a short while the girls had brushed their clothes, washed the dirt from their hands and faces, and combed their hair.

Jean gaily stood up for inspection. "Mrs. Strong, do I look presentable enough to approach Deputy Sheriff Alt?"

The ranchwoman laughed. "Of course. He's quite young, by the way, Jean, and unmarried. But don't get any ideas in your head!"

They all climbed into the jeep and ate lunch as they rode along. An hour later they reached Huntersville. This town was considerably larger than Rawhide and had a fair number of stores.

"The deputy sheriff's office is over there," said Mrs. Strong, pointing to a small wooden building. "I hope you'll find him in. Suppose your Aunt Harriet and I do a little shopping while you're talking to him. We'll meet back at the jeep in an hour."

She parked, and the girls immediately went to the office. Fortunately, Deputy Alt was there. Louise and Jean introduced themselves and told where they were staying. Then Louise described the finding of the dinosaur fossil.

"Great!" said the tall, slender, bronzed young man. "It's usually only archaeologists who make such discoveries. You can feel pretty set up, Miss Dana."

Louise blushed. "I suppose it should be reported

to your Department of Natural Resources," she said. "Would you mind doing it?"

"I'll be glad to," Deputy Alt replied, and added with a chuckle, "They'll probably give you some kind of citation."

"Oh, goodness! I don't want anything like that," Louise burst out, embarrassed. "Please, don't even tell the department who made the discovery."

"What!" the deputy sheriff was amazed.

Jean understood her sister's feeling, but she thought Louise was being entirely too modest. Laughing, she said, "Just don't let them hang up a solid gold plaque with my sister's name on it!"

"All right, I promise." Deputy Alt grinned. "But I think you deserve recognition for your discovery. This reptile, if authentic, is one hundred and twenty million years old. Back in those days," he went on, "this area wasn't the Rocky Mountains. It was a huge plain that extended all the way from central Utah to the Mississippi River.

"Some scientists believe the climate was tropical then, and part of the land full of thick, lush vegetation. This indicated swamps, where some of the dinosaur family liked to live. Most of them were vegetarians. I understand it took half a ton of fodder a day to keep a big one alive."

"How utterly amazing!" said Louise. "It's hard to believe the Rocky Mountains weren't always here. How did they originate?"

"They were formed from volcanoes," replied the deputy sheriff. "One explanation of why so many dinosaurs died at once is that they were suffocated by volcanic ash."

The officer went on to say that sections of the vast area once had been sand. Wind had heaped up huge piles which eventually hardened into sandstone.

"Why," queried Jean, "did dinosaurs need such long legs if they lived in swamps?"

"To eat from the treetops. Also, the creatures carried such tremendous weight in their bodies and sank in so deeply, they needed long legs to reach the bottom of the muck and still keep their torsos above it. We know that one branch of the family, the diplodocus, must have lived in areas of the swamp because they breathed through the top of their heads, so they could submerge and still get air. But many breeds used nostrils."

The deputy sheriff abruptly stopped speaking about dinosaurs and asked, "May I inquire how you girls happen to be visiting here?"

Jean told him that they were the girls who had been transporting a valuable shepherd dog from San Francisco to New York. "You've been alerted to be on the lookout for Baron, and the horse thieves too?"

"Yes," Deputy Alt replied. "But our men have not seen any sign of the dog or the two men."

"We're still hoping to locate Baron," Jean went

on. "From a few clues we've picked up, we wonder if he went toward Lost Lake."

Louise added, "We've heard about the witch who lives there. Some people say she's no longer around and others feel she's still at the lake. Have you heard anything?"

"I'm sure she's there," the deputy sheriff stated. "She was in town shopping just two days ago."

"Is her name, by any chance, Blanche Carmino?" Louise asked.

"I suspect it is," Deputy Alt replied. "The woman has never denied it when questioned on the subject. On the other hand, she has never admitted it. She sells her artifacts and makes purchases with almost no conversation."

Alt went on to say that the witch was often taunted by small boys and some cowboys. "I've been called several times to defend her. A few rascally kids in town like to pull her long hair. The cowboys walk behind her chanting rather uncomplimentary verses."

"How mean!" Louise exclaimed.

"Yes, it is," Alt agreed. "So far, the witch has always ignored her tormentors, but I'm afraid she'll get fed up someday and retaliate."

"How?" Jean asked.

"I've been told she's very handy with a gun," the deputy sheriff stated. "I assume she carries one, although it must be hidden in her pocket."

"I understand," said Jean, "that the witch

doesn't come to town often, so there's probably no chance of our seeing her today. I wish we had been here the other day when she was shopping. I'd like so much to talk to her."

"In place of that, why don't you girls walk two blocks up to the little historical museum in our school? They have some old photographs of the settlement of Pueblo Lake and letters to local residents from people who lived there before the great landslide."

"We'll do that," said Louise, "and thanks a million."

The girls said good-by and hurried off. "We'll just have time for a quick tour," Louise remarked as they reached the school.

Inside, the sisters found the museum room and at once went over to a long showcase. This contained pictures and letters which were spread out and easy to scrutinize.

The settlement must have been attractive and cozy, nestled at the foot of the mountain and facing the lake, Louise observed. The girls read and reread every word of the letters, looking intently for the name Carmino. But again their hopes of learning anything about the family were dashed. No one had mentioned them in the correspondence.

"It almost seems," said Louise, "as if Antonio Carmino was doing some kind of secret work. That's why there is no record of it any place."

"What in the world could it have been?" Jean asked. "Was he an archaeologist or geologist?"

The sisters returned to the jeep and found Aunt Harriet and Mrs. Strong already there. Louise and Jean reported their conversation with the deputy sheriff and also their trip to the museum.

"We think," said Louise, "that the witch's real name is Blanche Carmino. Her father was Antonio Carmino, but we didn't find any clue as to what kind of work he did. If only we could learn that, we might have a good clue to solving the secret of Lost Lake and what those people we've seen are trying to find."

Aunt Harriet had been gazing thoughtfully into space. Presently she turned to her nieces, and said, "Somewhere, sometime, some place I've heard that name—Antonio Carmino."

Instantly Louise and Jean became excited. "Oh, where?" Jean asked.

"I just cannot remember right this minute."

"Please try hard!" Louise begged her aunt.

CHAPTER XI

Pursuit

THE Dana sisters and Mrs. Strong sat quietly in the jeep, eagerly hoping that Aunt Harriet could recall where she had heard the name Antonio Carmino. Miss Dana thought and thought, but without success.

"Even if I did remember," she said, "the name might have nothing to do with this Carmino or his daughter Blanche. I think you girls had better not depend on me for a clue."

"The answer probably will come to you in the middle of the night," Mrs. Strong remarked. She smiled. "When the conscious mind is asleep, the subconscious often comes to the forefront."

Aunt Harriet laughed. "Tonight when I go to sleep, I'll tell that second mind of mine to get to work!"

Louise asked Mrs. Strong if she was in a hurry to return home. When she said she was not, the young sleuth suggested that they interview various people in Huntersville to see if anyone could supply information about the Carminos who had lived at Pueblo Lake.

"All right," Mrs. Strong agreed. "I suggest you and Jean start with the shopkeepers."

The women decided to wait in the jeep, so the girls hopped out and hurried up the street. Their first stop was the barbershop. The man in charge there gave them no help.

Next, the sisters went to a market, and then to a small department store. None of the people they queried at either place knew as much about the tragedy of Lost Lake as the girls did themselves, or had ever heard the name Carmino.

The first break came when Louise and Jean spoke to the town's druggist. He was a middle-aged, rotund man. While he could tell nothing about the inhabitants of Pueblo Lake, he referred the girls to an old-time resident, Mrs. Parker.

"She's a widow—lives in the last house on the outskirts of Huntersville to the west," said the kind-faced pharmacist.

The Danas thanked him and went out to the street. It was only a short distance to Mrs. Parker's house.

The elderly woman herself opened the door when they knocked. She was sweet-faced and friendly, and instantly invited the girls to make themselves comfortable in the living room. During the conversation which followed, they learned that Mrs. Parker was ninety years old, but still robust and clear thinking. Much to the surprise of the Danas, she did not inquire why the girls had come to call. Instead, she talked volubly about her fine family.

Louise and Jean nodded politely as they heard about one son of Mrs. Parker's being a doctor in Seattle, another a lawyer in New York, and that "my baby girl lives here."

"Yes, my daughter Ruth is mighty good to me," Mrs. Parker went on. "She's a widow and keeps house for me. She's at the market right now. Maybe you saw her—Ruth is tall and slender, and real pretty."

At last an opening came in the one-sided conversation for Jean to interject the subject of the secret of Lost Lake.

"It was dreadful—very dreadful." Mrs. Parker's face grew solemn. "My husband and I came here to live a short while before the landslide because of friends out there. All of them were lost." A tear trickled down the old woman's cheek.

Louise and Jean told her they had seen pictures and read accounts of the catastrophe. "It must have been terrible," Louise said sympathetically.

"Did you know an Antonio Carmino who lived there?" Jean asked.

Mrs. Parker's eyes lighted up. "Indeed I did. He was handsome and very dashing."

"He had a family?" Jean pursued the subject.

"Oh my, yes," Mrs. Parker replied. "A very pretty wife and a daughter. Her name was Blanche. I never saw her because she was in New York studying at an art school."

"Do you think the woman who lives out at Lost Lake now and is called 'the witch' could be Blanche Carmino?" Louise inquired.

"Possibly," Mrs. Parker answered. "One story has gone around that when Blanche returned from New York after the disaster, she went to pieces entirely, and left this area suddenly. No one here knew where she went. Several years later a strange woman came into town on a horse to shop. She would never give her name, nor say where she lived. I've always suspected the woman was Blanche Carmino and that she hadn't been able to make a living with her artwork."

Suddenly Louise and Jean recalled the echoing words they had heard, "Beautiful artwork." If the witch of Lost Lake was Blanche Carmino, could she have spoken them?

"But that echo was deep," Louise reflected, "as if it had been a man's voice."

"Whoever the witch is," said Mrs. Parker, "it's generally conceded around here that she's a bit daft. If she is Blanche, no doubt the tragedy affected her mind."

"That could be the case," said Louise. "It's a terrible shame to think of such a thing happening."

"Yes, it is," the old woman agreed. "A nice young girl like that, to suffer so much. And it seems to me, from what I hear, that all the folks around here do is annoy Blanche and make fun of her."

Louise smiled. "Not everybody," she said. "Just mischievous youngsters and some thoughtless cowboys."

"What do you suppose the woman is doing out at Lost Lake?" Mrs. Parker asked.

"That's what my sister and I are trying to find out," Jean replied. "We understand she does a lot of digging. Maybe she's hunting for something valuable."

"You mean those old Indian artifacts?" Mrs. Parker asked.

"Perhaps," Louise answered. "On the other hand, the witch may be hunting for something that was buried by the landslide."

"Like what?" Mrs. Parker queried. "For nearly a year after that landslide, human vultures were out there digging up everything they could. It was disgusting!"

Louise and Jean felt they had learned all they could from Mrs. Parker and had stayed long enough, anyway. They thanked her profusely for her information and rose to leave.

"If we ever have a chance to talk to the witch," said Louise at the doorway, "we'll certainly try to help her."

"Bless you for that!" Mrs. Parker smiled, and waved as the Danas went off down the street.

The girls walked back toward the jeep. Jean's eyes twinkled. "Since Antonio Carmino was a handsome dashing man, maybe that will help Aunt Harriet's memory!"

The sisters giggled, and as soon as they saw Miss Dana, put the question to her. "Handsome? Dashing?" Again Aunt Harriet thought hard, but finally she shook her head. "No. Even the description doesn't jog my memory. I've concluded that I must have heard of Antonio Carmino by reputation, whoever he is, and that I never met the man."

"You know," said Jean, heaving a sigh, "I'm dying of thirst. Why don't we all have a soda before we start back to the ranch?"

"Good idea," Louise agreed.

The group had just stepped away from the jeep when Louise happened to glance at a car speeding past. Her heart almost stood still.

"There go the Rineharts!" she exclaimed, and tried to get the license number but failed.

"We must chase them!" Jean cried out.

Aunt Harriet wanted to go for the deputy sheriff and tell him.

"But we'll lose time!" Jean said urgently. "After all, those two stole Jubilee!"

Mrs. Strong was convinced. "Jump in!" she said. "It's bad luck to let a thief out of your sight!"

The doors of the jeep were quickly slammed shut and the chase began. Whether the couple had recognized the Dana girls or whether they were just in a hurry, the pursuers did not know. In any case, Sam and Sally Rinehart were now driving at top speed.

"Don't let them get out of sight!" Louise begged.

Mrs. Strong drove away from town as fast as she dared. Aunt Harriet, bouncing around as they sped along the rough surface, cried out, "W-we sh-shouldn't be g-going so fast! The s-sheriff should be chasing the thieves!"

CHAPTER XII

The Unfriendly Ewe

"I WONDER if the car belongs to the Rineharts or if they stole that too," said Jean, who was seated next to her sister in the back of the jeep.

"I'd certainly like to find out," said Louise. "Where do you suppose they're going?" she asked, watching the road ahead carefully.

"I wish I knew." Jean frowned. "I'm mad at myself for not getting the license number. Did you get it?"

Louise shook her head. "No, isn't that awful? Everything happened so fast. The car was too far away before I realized who was in it."

The road twisted and turned, past occasional patches of woods. At some points, it was hugged by hills and canyons. At last Mrs. Strong reached a long open stretch. The Rineharts' car had vanished!

"What luck!" Jean said in disappointment. "Where could they have gone?"

"Actually there are many hiding places off this road," said Mrs. Strong. "It's my guess the Rineharts knew we were after them and pulled in among some trees or followed the curve of a canyon until their car was out of sight."

The Danas were dismayed to have had their quarry in plain view, only to lose track of the couple altogether.

Mrs. Strong, surprisingly, began to laugh. "Forgive me, please," she said. "I'm sorry we didn't capture those people, but I just got to thinking—this is the most excitement I've had in years!"

Aunt Harriet sighed. "I'm glad you're enjoying it. If I had my way, I'd like a little slower pace on such a rough road!"

Louise and Jean looked at each other. Did they dare suggest that the group make a search of the woods and canyon? Before the girls had a chance to bring up the subject, Mrs. Strong said:

"I wish I could continue the search for the Rineharts, but I really must get home in time for the evening chores and to feed my animals. You know, it's bad luck to leave a pet that depends on you—he may turn on you when you do show up —I suppose it's because of his being too hungry."

The Danas did not comment. Mrs. Strong was truly a contradiction, they thought. She was brave and seemed willing to undertake any difficult task to help others. Yet she was certainly influenced by her superstitions!

As they rode along, this time at a more comfortable rate of speed, the ranchwoman said she would stop in Rawhide to report seeing the Rineharts. When they reached the town, she asked the girls to go into the general store and telephone Deputy Sheriff Alt from there. The sisters hopped out of the jeep and went inside.

Caleb Winthrop said he would be happy to have them use his telephone. Louise gave the deputy a full report and was assured his men would be alerted.

It was late afternoon when the travellers reached the ranch. Mr. Strong met them as they pulled up to the house. He wore a broad grin. "Well, folks," he said, "I trust you had a successful trip."

When Louise and Jean told the story of their recent adventures, he whistled in amazement. Then, with a chuckle, he asked, "Do you girls *ever* spend a quiet day?"

"Not when we're trying to solve a couple of mysteries at once!" Jean replied, grinning.

The rancher announced he had news of his own. "It may be very good, too," he said. "One of my herders who arrived a little while ago from our farthest fence says he saw a dog that fits Baron's description."

"Oh, how marvellous!" Louise cried out. "Where?"

"I'll show you on a map I have of the ranch," Mr. Strong offered, and went on, "The dog wouldn't come near my man, even though he called him by name. That could mean, of course, that it wasn't Baron, but another German shepherd. I have a hunch, though, it was Baron, because during the time I've lived here, I've never heard of anyone around owning a German shepherd!"

"Would it be possible for us to go out there and look around?" Jean asked hopefully.

"Why, sure thing," Mr. Strong replied. "Let's talk about it at supper. Right now, there's a lot of work to do and it's getting late."

Remembering what Mrs. Strong had said about feeding her pets, Louise and Jean offered to do this. The ranchwoman accepted, but added laughingly, "First I'll go speak to each one. They expect it."

After she had done so, Mrs. Strong went into the house to prepare supper.

Meanwhile, the girls fed the chickens and collected the eggs. Next, they brought food to the dog Eleanor, to the fawn, which arrived for his evening meal, the eagle with the broken wing, and the lazy old tomcat.

"They don't seem to mind *who* feeds them," Jean said with a giggle, "as long as they eat!"

As soon as supper was finished and the dishes had been washed, Mr. Strong spread his map out on the dining-room table.

"I had no idea your ranch was so large," Aunt Harriet commented, and Jean asked, "Do you have sheep over the entire place?"

"Oh, no," Mr. Strong answered. "We give the grazing lands a rest and move the sheep to new fields." He put his finger on a spot at the rim of the ranch. "Here's where the herder saw the dog he thought might be Baron."

"How far is that from here?" Louise asked eagerly.

Mr. Strong smiled. "As a matter of fact, it's on the way to Lost Lake."

"It is!" Jean exclaimed. "Then Baron could have been held by the witch, and escaped!"

"I don't know whether this is a good or a bad clue," Louise said. "If Baron isn't at Lost Lake, there's no telling what direction he may have taken."

"Just the same," Jean declared, "I'd like to hunt for him from the spot where he was seen."

"Oh, I would too!" Louise assured her sister.

Mr. Strong looked at Aunt Harriet, then at the girls. "I've arranged my work so that day after tomorrow, Monday, I can inspect the sheep in that section. I want to select the ones that are ready for market. Would you girls like to go there with me, and after I've finished, continue on to Lost Lake?"

The sisters were thrilled. But Louise asked,

"Won't you have to bring the sheep back to send them to market?"

"My boys will drive them in," he said cheerfully. "Don't worry. We'll go on to Lost Lake."

"Wonderful!" Jean's face glowed.

Mr. Strong chuckled. "I guess Mom here and your Aunt Harriet will be glad to have us out of the way for a while. It'll give 'em a chance to finish that hooked rug!"

Early the following morning the girls were awakened by the whinnying of a horse. They leaped up and peered from their window.

"It's Jubilee!" Jean cried. "She's back! She broke loose from those awful Rineharts!"

"Or maybe they got scared and let her loose," Louise guessed. "Anyway, she's home!"

"Hi, Jubilee!" Jean called, poking her head out the window. "I'll be right down!"

The girls pulled on Levis, coats, and boots, then rushed outdoors. Jean hugged the lovable saddle horse, while Louise patted her affectionately. As they were leading the mare to the barn, Mr. Strong came from the ranch house.

"Well, I'll be sheep-dyed!" he exclaimed. "Where did you come from?"

Jubilee nuzzled her owner, who went with the girls to the horse's stall. Ginger gave a low whinny of welcome to her stablemate.

Jean said exuberantly, "Now I'll have my own horse to ride tomorrow!"

That evening the girls packed the food, water containers, and beverages for the trip and went to bed early. The first one ready the next day was Eleanor. From past experience the dog knew when preparations were underway to round up sheep for market, and she would have a big part in this operation.

"Eleanor is one of my best herders," said Mr. Strong as the riders gathered after breakfast with their own mounts and a pack horse. "Those sheep will pay attention to her when we men are having a hard time with them."

Louise went to speak to the sheep dog. "Eleanor, if you're that smart, how about finding Baron for us?"

The dog wagged her tail vigorously and whined softly as if agreeing to undertake the task.

"Mount up!" the rancher called.

The girls swung onto Ginger and Jubilee, waved gaily to Aunt Harriet and Mrs. Strong, then rode off with the rancher. The way led over rolling country almost free of buttes and canyons. They made excellent time and by midmorning could see a great flock of sheep ahead. Each animal had a green circle painted just above its stumpy tail, to indicate the sheep belonged to the Strong ranch.

"Goodness!" said Jean. "I had no idea you raised so many!"

Mr. Strong grinned boyishly. "We send a couple of thousand to market every year. I daresay some of the lamb may have reached your own home-town butcher shops."

As they drew closer the girls could see several sheepherders riding horses among the animals.

Mr. Strong leaned down from his saddle and said to Eleanor, "Go get Juan!"

Without hesitation, the dog bounded off and a few minutes later brought back Juan Desido. The Mexican foreman said good morning to the group, then added, "Señor Strong, how many sheep you want for market?"

"I have an order for two hundred and fifty," the rancher replied. "A carload."

Juan grinned broadly, his tiny mustache stretching out almost to twice its length. "That will be easy job."

Mr. Strong and the girls dismounted, but the rancher suggested that Louise and Jean stay where they were and watch. "Come on, Eleanor!"

The two men and the dog walked among the flock and work began. With practiced eyes Mr. Strong selected the sheep he wanted. As soon as he had made his choice, Juan or one of the other sheepherders painted a red circle on its rump.

"This is really an interesting sight, isn't it?" Louise remarked as she looked at the sheep—some standing still, some walking about slowly and munching the partly dried grass.

Jean giggled. "They look better from a distance.

Close up they're pretty dirty. No white, woolly lambs here!"

"I suppose all the animals that go to market will be sheared," said Louise, "and meet their doom without the fur coats!"

Jean did not reply with one of her usual quips. She had strolled over to a young ewe standing protectively near a lamb, probably one of her own.

"Aren't they cute?" Jean called to her sister.

She leaned down and pulled up a handful of grass. Walking forward, she held out her hand toward the animals. The pair came up to her and the ewe grabbed at the grass. Jean, thinking that the mother sheep was gentle, began to stroke the young lamb. Instantly the ewe gave the girl a gentle butt. Jean laughed and tried again to pet the lamb. This time the ewe lowered her head, shoving the girl aside.

"What's the big idea?" Jean said, giggling. "So you want to play games? How about a ride?"

She climbed astride the ewe's back. Instantly the animal started to run. Jean pulled up her knees, sank her hands deep into the woolly back, and hung on tightly.

"Whoa! Stop!" she commanded. "I'll get off!"

From a distance Mr. Strong and Juan heard Jean cry out and turned to look. The sight of the ewe gamboling about with Jean riding on her back caused them to roar with laughter. Louise, too, was enjoying the show, but a moment later her smile froze into a look of fright. The ewe's hind legs had gone up high and Jean went sailing through the air. She landed with a thud on the grass!

Louise rushed up to her sister, who lay dazed for a moment. Then she sat up, smiling ruefully. "I'm all right," Jean said. "I guess it served me right."

By this time Mr. Strong and Juan had run over. As Jean rose to her feet, the rancher asked how she felt.

Jean managed a smile. "As if I'd been put in my place," she replied. "The Strong sheep sure are *strong!*"

"They're not used to human playmates," said Mr. Strong. Chuckling, he and Juan went off to continue the selecting of sheep. The girls waited patiently at the fringe of the flock. Finally the rancher joined them, saying his work was complete. The riders mounted and he led the way around the edge of the grazing ground. Presently they came to a woods.

All this time Eleanor had been following them. Now Mr. Strong reined up and looked at her. "You want to go along, don't you, old girl?" he asked.

At that moment the dog suddenly pricked up her ears. Then she growled and like a shot was off into the woods.

"She must have heard some animal," Mr. Strong explained.

"You mean one that's an enemy to sheep?" Jean asked.

"Yes. Perhaps a mountain lion!"

Suddenly Louise had another idea. She asked excitedly, "Do you suppose it could be Baron?"

She jumped from her horse and ran into the woods after Eleanor.

CHAPTER XIII

Mountain Lion!

WHEN Jean saw her sister dash into the woods, she instantly raced after her. Jean could not see the sheep dog Eleanor, but apparently Louise did.

The chase among the trees was a rough one. Roots, vines, and upjutting stones impeded the girls' progress time and again. They turned their ankles as they stepped into unseen holes. But both of them kept on running, hoping each second to spot the missing German shepherd dog.

Suddenly Eleanor stopped in her tracks. First Louise, then Jean caught up to her. There was not a sound from any animal in the woods, though they listened intently for several seconds.

"What made the noise Eleanor heard?" Louise asked her sister finally. "For a while I thought we'd find Baron, maybe being cowed by some large animal."

"I had my doubts," said Jean. "Baron isn't the kind of dog who'd run away. He'd stand his ground and fight!"

"You're right," Louise agreed. "But—" She paused and pointed. "Look!" Louise whispered, gazing straight ahead of her.

A man was furtively and hurriedly slipping off among the trees. Eleanor made no move to go after him and this puzzled the Danas. If the man was what the dog was after, why was she no longer interested?

"Maybe he was trying to steal a sheep," Louise said. "Anyway, if Eleanor was chasing him, she may think he is far enough away by now and doesn't intend any harm."

The girls scrutinized the area, but detected no further sign of the stranger's presence. Finally the Danas turned and slowly started back toward the spot where they had entered the woods.

"That man," said Louise, "surely acted suspiciously. Do you suppose he has something to do with Baron's disappearance?"

"It's possible," Jean said.

Eleanor was trotting on, keeping a short distance in front of the girls. Whenever she went through an especially tangled part of the woods, the girls would try to skirt the area. At once she would bound after them and bark furiously, as if telling them they were not going in the right direction. Smiling, the Danas would take the cue.

"Much more of this and our clothes will be torn to shreds!" Jean complained.

"Better that than to be lost," Louise said. "We mustn't keep Mr. Strong waiting. And besides, we're on our way to Lost Lake, remember?"

Jean grinned. "How could I forget?"

The girls had just come to a particularly dense section of the woods when Eleanor suddenly stopped, looked up, then began to growl and bark furiously.

"Now what does she see?" Jean asked, glancing upward also.

The next second terror seized her and Louise as well. A large mountain lion was crouched on a tree limb directly ahead, ready to spring down upon them!

The big cat was spitting and snarling. The sisters were defenseless, with no weapon of any kind. They were almost hypnotized, expecting the deadly onslaught at any moment.

The lion hesitated, however, apparently because of the furiously barking dog who by now seemed like anything but the friendly animal the Danas knew. Eleanor was wild and her eyes blazed as she jumped around.

Suddenly Louise realized that the dog was holding the big cat at bay in order to give the girls time to make a getaway. She quickly told Jean this and said:

"Let's run!"

Jean needed no urging. "Just the same, I feel like a heel leaving Eleanor. She may be attacked herself! Oh, I wish I could do something to help her!"

"We'll get Mr. Strong!" Louise suggested, and doubled her pace.

The girls fairly flew out of the woods and almost ran full tilt into the rancher, who had sensed trouble. Quickly they explained that Eleanor's life was in danger from the mountain lion.

Rifle in hand, Mr. Strong ran off among the trees, following the direction from which the barking came.

Louise and Jean stood stock-still, their eyes closed to shut out the picture of the tragic scene which might be taking place. Could Mr. Strong reach Eleanor in time to save the faithful sheep dog?

A minute later they heard a shot ring out. Jean said in a quivering voice, "I guess Mr. Strong got the mountain lion, but I hope Eleanor is all right."

Louise was too worried even to answer. She simply stared until she saw Mr. Strong come crashing through the underbrush. A second later the girls' hearts leaped with joy. Eleanor ran from the woods unharmed!

"What a heroine you are!" Louise cried, and leaned down to hug the brave sheep dog. "You saved our lives!"

Mr. Strong, too, was a bit unnerved by the close call the Danas had had, and said that if any harm had come to them, he never would be able to forgive himself.

"I should have followed you," he declared, "since I know there are mountain lions around."

"Please, it's not your fault," Louise assured him. "Jean and I rushed off so quickly you didn't have time to warn us. Did—did you get the mountain lion?" she asked.

"Yes. He'll never bother any sheep again." The rancher's good humour returned. "I should have brought the skin back so one of you could have a trophy to show your friends back home."

"No, thanks," Jean said quickly. "It would be too much of a reminder of the scare we've just had."

"Scare or no scare, I'm hungry," Mr. Strong announced. "How about our having lunch now before we go on?"

As they ate, Louise and Jean told him about the man they had seen in the woods. The rancher frowned. "Trying to steal a lamb, no doubt," he said. "That is one reason we have Eleanor. She's a marvel at spotting rustlers, human or animal."

Despite his theory, the girls could not help but wonder if the man they had glimpsed could have been Sam Rinehart, Ben Hopley, or Chet Simpson. So far, these people had been unaccounted for since their disappearances. The mysterious man might have been a spy rather than a rustler.

"You're finding our country mysterious and

dangerous and rather wild," Mr. Strong remarked to the Danas. "If you want to discontinue our ride to Lost Lake, just say so and we'll go back to the ranch."

"We wouldn't dream of such a thing!" Louise declared stoutly. "It gives me the shivers to think of what may have happened to Baron, but if it's possible to find out where he is, dead or alive, I'll feel better."

"Yes," said Jean, "and I haven't given up hope that he's all right."

As the three searchers mounted their horses, Eleanor stood nearby. She whined and wagged her tail as if begging to go.

"Can't we take her along?" Louise asked. "After doing such a good deed, she ought to have some fun!"

The rancher smiled. "Eleanor is a working dog. Her place is here. You've already seen firsthand evidence of how valuable she is. Eleanor will have her fun some other time."

There was little conversation as the riders moved beyond the bounds of the Strong ranch and set off in a direct line for Lost Lake. The scenery was similar to what the girls had seen on their other trip, though more rugged. Travelling became difficult, and they made rather slow progress, but continued riding for several hours without a halt.

Finally Mr. Strong called, "A few miles ahead is a cave where we'll spend the night. It's sheltered and contains some interesting pictographs. They're very well preserved and different from the petroglyphs you saw—some of these are humorous."

Jean grinned. "Sounds like an interesting Indian motel!"

Just before the trio came to the cave area, Louise, who was in the lead, called back, "Somebody else has been here and not long ago. There are horseshoe prints and those of a man's boots. He must have been leading his horse."

Hearing this, Mr. Strong said he had better ride ahead of the girls. The Danas reined up and let him pass them. They had just entered a canyon, which was most picturesque, but the beauty of the place was secondary in the minds of the riders. All were worried about what they might meet ahead.

The prints showed that the horse and the man had plodded straight along. But suddenly the marks turned sharp right.

"They lead directly to the cave!" Mr. Strong informed the girls. "You stay here while I go find out if anybody is around."

The girls waited anxiously, with Louise watching Mr. Strong, and Jean keeping an eye on the rocky bench above the cave. She could see nothing but the bare outjutting formation.

The rancher called from inside, "No one here! Come on!"

The girls rode forward and dismounted. They hitched their horses and walked into the cave, which had such a large opening the light penetrated far back into it.

"Ugh!" Jean grimaced upon seeing the floor, untidy and littered with fresh scraps of food to which bushy-tailed wood rats were helping themselves!

"That man whose prints we were following was staying here!" Louise said tensely. "And not long ago!"

She and Jean felt uneasy. Who was the stranger? Would he come back? Was he a friendly person or one of the thieves they were still eager to catch?

CHAPTER XIV

A Substitute Guard

THE two girl sleuths carefully examined the footprints of the unknown man who had been in the cave. After a few minutes they came back and made a report to Mr. Strong.

"The stranger came here," Louise said, "left his horse outside the cave, and later rode off in the opposite direction to the one from which we came."

The rancher surveyed the marks himself, then commented, "The man went straight toward Lost Lake, but this may not mean a thing. He could have gone for water or he may be hunting—perhaps for a rabbit or a woodchuck for his supper. There's no telling when he may return."

"What makes you think he expects to return, Mr. Strong?" Jean inquired.

"Because night will be coming on and this cave provides good shelter."

Louise and Jean did not contradict the rancher, but felt it was just as logical that the man had travelled a good distance from the spot by this time. If so, he might have no intention of returning.

"If he is one of the thieves," Louise thought, "I hope there's no surprise attack. At least we're fore-warned."

Mr. Strong spoke up. "As I told you girls, this was where I planned we would camp for the night." He shrugged. "I suppose we still can. But I'll stay on watch just inside the cave."

"Oh, you need some sleep, too," Louise said solicitously. "How about our taking turns standing guard?"

The rancher was reluctant to allow this for reasons of safety or fear of a surprise attack. The girls laughingly assured him that in case anyone showed up, they could yell loudly enough to wake him up immediately! Finally he consented to the arrangement.

"Come on, Louise," Jean urged cheerfully. "Let's clean up our home for the night!"

The Danas set to work and began by picking up the many pieces of paper on the cavern floor. Suddenly the girls discovered that there were printed words on the scraps revealing the contents and weight of various packages of food.

Jean exclaimed excitedly, "These are bits of labels!" She called to Mr. Strong, who was outside tending to the horses. When he entered, Jean said, "Maybe you'll recognize some of these labels and they'll give us a clue to the person who was using this cave."

She and Louise smoothed out the crumpled bits and spread them on the ground. Then, as if working a jigsaw puzzle, the girls began putting them together. Mr. Strong watched with interest.

Suddenly he said, "Good for you! See what that part of a label says? Dora Ann's Market—in Huntersville! The man who stayed here purchased supplies in Huntersville. If we go there, maybe we can find out who the fellow is."

Several other larger scraps, when put together, formed a bag with the imprinted name: Huntersville Drug Store.

"What I can't understand," said Mr. Strong, "is why the man who was here bothered to tear up these papers."

"Because he didn't want anybody to know where he had been," Jean guessed. "That definitely makes him a suspect."

Louise nodded. "It strikes me that he isn't extremely bright. If he really wanted to cover his tracks, he would have burned these papers."

Mr. Strong laughed. "I just happened to think— maybe some wood rats chewed these papers apart."

Louise and Jean picked up the scraps and examined them thoroughly. "No teeth marks,"

Louise reported. "These papers must have been torn by human hands."

As soon as the cave floor had been tidied, the Danas turned their full attention to the pictographs lining the walls. Many of them were similar in subject to the petroglyphs which the girls had seen.

Mr. Strong pointed to several humorous scenes. One of these showed the figure of a man being thrown high into the air by an angry buck.

Louise giggled. "Jean, you ought to appreciate this scene! Looks as if he may be one of your ancestors!" she teased.

Jean laughed good-naturedly. "That makes him one of *your* ancestors, too, don't forget!" she countered, then added, "I didn't realize my thrilling ride on the ewe today was history repeating itself!"

Louise chortled. "And here we are about to sleep in our ancestor's cave!"

The three companions continued to walk around, admiring the other pictures. All of a sudden Jean said tensely:

"Listen! I hear something outside!"

Both Danas and Mr. Strong rushed to the opening of the cave. The two girls burst into laughter but Mr. Strong looked provoked. In front of them stood Eleanor, wagging her tail happily.

"You old maverick!" Mr. Strong cried. "Eleanor, you know where you belong—back doing your job of protecting our sheep or else at home guarding the ranch house! Why did you follow us?"

The dog looked crestfallen. She sat down on her haunches and hung her head dejectedly. The Danas felt sorry for the faithful animal.

"Maybe," said Louise, "Eleanor figured *we* need protection more than the sheep or the ranch house."

Jean agreed. "Of course she did!"

Mr. Strong thought over this idea. Then he smiled and said, "You have a point, girls. Well, we'll give Eleanor the benefit of the doubt. Since she's here, we'll appoint her guard and we'll all get some rest."

As soon as the sheep dog realized she was not going to be sent home, she perked up. Then Eleanor began sniffing about the place.

"I'll bet she's picking up the scent of the stranger who was here," Jean surmised.

A little later the travellers decided it was time for supper. First, the horses were given some oats and allowed to graze a bit. Mr. Strong had found a stream trickling down over the rock wall and led the thirsty animals to it for a drink.

The girls, meanwhile, gave Eleanor some meat from the sandwiches. Afterward, the dog went off to hunt on her own. Finally the girls and the rancher ate, then decided to stretch out in their sleeping bags.

Eleanor returned and lay down at the opening of

the cave, seemingly asleep, but the others knew she was alert to every sound. Louise and Jean, weary from their long ride, fell into deep slumber and did not awaken until the sun arose.

Mr. Strong was already outside. He had fed the animals and packed his sleeping bag onto the pack horse. The girls prepared an appetizing breakfast of bacon, powdered scrambled eggs, biscuits, and tomato juice. Before they began to eat, Jean slipped a piece of bacon to Eleanor.

"You're a wonderful guard," she said, patting the dog's shaggy head.

"I don't know what to do about her," said the rancher. "Maybe we should take Eleanor along. On the other hand, she's really needed back at the ranch."

Eleanor cocked her head, then gobbled a second piece of bacon Jean gave her. The dog gave a little whine and a short bark, then turned and ran off in the direction of the ranch. Louise and Jean marveled aloud at the dog's intuition.

Mr. Strong grinned. "Yes—she understands what I want," he said. "I'd be lost without her."

The three riders soon were in the saddle to continue their trip. About an hour later they came to a breathtakingly beautiful canyon. The girls reined up to look at the colourful, odd-shaped walls and the noisy, bubbling stream which rushed along at the side of the trail.

"I shall never forget this scenery!" Jean remarked. "It's terrific!"

Louise was about to make a comment when suddenly, seemingly out of nowhere, came a loud, deep voice. It commanded:

"Go no farther! Turn back if you value your lives!"

The startled riders looked all around but there was no sign of the man who had spoken. The strange order was not repeated.

Puzzled, Louise asked, "What do you make of it?"

"I don't know," Mr. Strong replied with concern. "But whoever gave the warning sounded as if he meant business!"

The rancher went on to say that he wondered whether he might be exposing the girls to more danger. "I really feel I haven't the right to do so," he said. "We'd better turn back and head for the ranch."

"And give up the hunt for Baron?" Jean was shocked by the suggestion.

At that instant a frisky squirrel ran directly in front of Ginger. The horse reared, and Louise was almost flung from the saddle. She managed to hang on, but when the horse came down on four feet, she bolted up the canyon from which they had just been warned to stay away!

Louise pulled hard on the reins but it had no

effect on the frightened horse. Ginger galloped faster than ever.

Jean and Mr. Strong immediately followed at full speed. Both were fearful that Louise might be thrown. Also, they were afraid she was headed for danger at the hands of the person who had called the strange warning!

CHAPTER XV

Arrow Escape

GINGER raced on with Louise clinging to the saddle horn with one hand, the reins in the other. In desperation the girl yanked up quickly on the reins, let them loose, then pulled them up short again. This unexpected manoeuvre slowed the run-away horse and she finally stopped.

"Don't scare me again like that, Ginger!" Louise said, catching her breath. Then she patted the horse's neck affectionately. "Surely it wasn't just that little squirrel which frightened you," she went on. "Horses are supposed to have a sixth sense. Something strange is going on here. I wish you could tell me what it is you know that I don't!"

Jean, Mr. Strong, and the pack horse caught up to Louise in a few moments. They were relieved to see that she was still astride her horse and un-harmed. The rancher agreed that Ginger had sensed some unseen danger from which she had tried to escape.

"I sure wish I knew *what* danger," Mr. Strong said in concern. "And where it is."

Jean added, "And I'd like to know more about that warning we heard. Maybe Ginger detected the scent of the person who gave it."

"That could be," Mr. Strong said. "And was the warning from a friend or an enemy—and what prompted it?"

The three riders had various theories. Mr. Strong thought possibly there was physical danger in the canyon, such as a threatened rockslide. Louise, recalling the previous explosion, suggested that perhaps a charge of dynamite was about to be set off at a quarry.

"It would have detonated by this time," Jean remarked. "Anyway, we would have heard the blast."

"I don't recall a quarry in this area," said Mr. Strong. "I think the warning was given by somebody who is trying to keep us away from here for a personal reason. I suggest we go on, but very cautiously. I know where there's a small branching canyon which leads to Lost Lake. We'll take that."

He added that the girls would find the small canyon a longer and rougher route. Louise and Jean assured him that they did not mind.

"Anything to avoid a dangerous lurking enemy!"

said Louise, who was still a bit shaken from her wild race on the runaway horse.

The three riders started off once more. Each kept looking alertly ahead, behind, and to left and right, both on the floor of the canyon and up at the benches atop the rocky walls. Mr. Strong had taken a pair of binoculars from his saddlebag and hung them around his neck. From time to time he used them, but neither he nor the girls saw anyone.

After a half hour's ride, Mr. Strong called out that the branching canyon was only a few yards ahead. "It's to the right. You can't miss it."

The group had advanced only a few feet when suddenly they were startled by an arrow shot from the bench. It whizzed through the air, directly in front of them, and landed quivering in a gravelly spot between two rocks in the canyon floor!

"Oh!" Louise and Jean cried out involuntarily.

The riders had reined up instantly, their hearts pounding. Would their unknown attacker shoot more arrows?

"Hug the wall!" Mr. Strong ordered, and the three urged their horses to the side. There was a slight overhang of rocks here which afforded some protection. They came to a halt and waited. No more arrows were shot into the canyon.

"The one which nearly got us could have been a stray," Mr. Strong suggested. "Maybe some bowman was deer hunting and missed."

Louise and Jean smiled ruefully. They were sure that the rancher was merely trying to allay any possible fears on their part. The girls did not contradict his theory, but both felt that the shooting of the arrow had been deliberate, and the sender was doing the same thing they were—playing a waiting game.

Finally Mr. Strong said, "I suggest we dismount and lead the horses. We'll stick close to the canyon wall and go ahead as planned. That way, anyone above us with itchy fingers on a bowstring can't reach us."

Fortunately, the overhang of the cliff extended for some distance and the trio proceeded in safety. The protective overhang eventually turned a corner into the branch canyon. As the three entered it single file, the girls gasped at the beauty ahead of them. The opening between the high multicoloured walls was little more than a gorge, with a shallow rock-filled stream twisting through it.

There was only a narrow strip of dry stony earth on the right side and the Danas realized that here and there it would be necessary for them to take their horses through the water in order to continue the trip.

"We'll have to be very careful where we lead Ginger and Jubilee, or one of them might break a leg," Louise observed to her sister.

At the point where the overhang ended, Mr. Strong told the girls to wait while he went ahead and made an investigation. "I want to avoid any more danger for you two," he said. "And for me, too," he added with a grin.

After ground-hitching his horse, he cautiously stepped into the open. Again using his binoculars, he swept the landscape for signs of any waiting attacker.

"I don't see a soul," he reported. "I think it's safe for us to go on."

Jean, in the lead, scrutinized the ground carefully so that Jubilee would not step into a hole or skid on a slippery rock. Every so often the girl and her companions would stop and gaze all around as a precaution against any furtive movements of an enemy. Still no one appeared and gradually the travellers' immediate fears left them.

It was during a pause to rest the horses that Jean noticed something unusual ahead. She led Jubilee on. Directly ahead on the narrow trail a crudely built ladder stood against the canyon wall. By the time the others reached Jean, she was staring in fascination at the rungs.

"These rungs are wet and muddy!" she exclaimed. "Somebody has climbed them recently!"

Louise asked Mr. Strong if anyone lived in the canyon. He shook his head. "Not that I know of. Long ago some Indians made their home here, I'm told, but they've been gone nearly a thousand years!"

The three riders speculated on the puzzle of the ladder. Who had put it there? Who was using it, and why?

"It might have been used by the person who shot that arrow," Jean suggested. "He may have known a shortcut to this spot and beat us here!"

"If that's the case," said Mr. Strong, "the bowman might not be an enemy. If he were on this bench above us, he could easily have heard our approach and shot another arrow."

"If the person using the ladder isn't waiting to harm us, what is he doing here?" Louise asked.

The rancher laughed. "I'd say he came down to get some water."

"But where did he take it?" Louise persisted.

"Your guess is as good as mine," Mr. Strong said. "He could be a hunter, a camper, or an archaeologist. Such people wander around the Rocky Mountains all the time."

"There's one way to find out," said Jean. "Go up the ladder and take a look."

"Don't forget our main job," Louise reminded her. "It's to reach Lost Lake and hunt for Baron. We'll use up precious time if we look around that bench."

Mr. Strong chuckled. " 'A house divided against itself,' eh?" he quoted. "Suppose I toss a coin to settle the argument."

He produced a twenty-five-cent piece and said, "Heads, we go right on to Lost Lake. If it's tails, you may have the pleasure of climbing that ladder, Jean. Okay?"

"Okay," the girls chorused.

The rancher tossed the coin into the air, caught it on the back of his hand, and covered it with the palm of his other hand. He waited and grinned at the Danas, creating suspense.

Finally Mr. Strong lifted his palm. "Jean, you win. The side with the eagle is face up!"

Laughing, Jean lost no time in climbing the ladder. The others waited breathlessly for her report. She stepped onto the rocky bench, then a few seconds later called down:

"Oh, this is amazing! Come on up! There are marvellous cliff dwellings just a little way from here in a giant pit!"

Excitedly Louise ascended the ladder. When she reached the top, Mr. Strong followed. Together, they walked to the edge of the pit for a closer look at the ruins. The ancient buildings were extensive, and though in a crumbling state, told the story that once this had been a very productive and prosperous Indian center.

"It looks like a whole village with a palace in the middle!" Louise noted.

Jean agreed, then began to laugh. "There's not a soul around. One of the Indian's ghosts must have been using that ladder!"

The words were hardly out of her mouth when the group suddenly saw a man step into the open from behind one of the circular-walled structures.

"We must find out who he is!" Louise said excitedly.

Mr. Strong called down to him in a loud voice. The man in the ruins looked up, startled.

CHAPTER XVI

Danger in the Rapids

THE man standing in the ancient ruins was about thirty years old, tall, blond, and attractive looking. Recovering from his surprise at seeing the Danas and Mr. Strong, he smiled.

"Hello there!" he called up from the pit. "You folks gave me a scare. Where did you all come from? I'm not used to having visitors in this remote spot!"

"We're from a ranch north of here," Mr. Strong said noncommittally.

The friendly stranger said he was Hal Compton, an archaeologist, from Atlanta, Georgia. "I'm writing a thesis for my Ph.D. on findings in dinosaur country."

"How fascinating!" Jean exclaimed. "And are you staying here?"

"Yes, I'm camping out. Do you all want to

come down and see what I've found?" Mr. Compton asked cordially.

He pointed to a crude ladder which reached into the pit. The others had not noticed it before because the ladder hugged the side and blended with the earth so well that it was inconspicuous.

"I'll go first," Mr. Strong offered, and after he had made the descent, the Danas quickly climbed down.

A closer look at Hal Compton's open friendly face helped assure them he was a person to be trusted. The rancher now introduced the sisters and himself to the archaeologist.

"By any chance, do you girls attend Starhurst boarding school?" he asked eagerly.

"Why, yes," Louise answered in amazement. "Do you know anyone at Starhurst?"

"I sure do," Hal said. "My kid sister, Amy, goes there. She has often spoken of you girls."

As he grinned, Jean could see the family resemblance. She cried out, "Of course—Amy Compton! She's a grand girl!"

"And a straight A student," Louise added.

Mr. Strong laughed. "Talk about a small world! We've just proved it." He now reminded the Danas they should look around quickly, then depart, because they still had many miles to cover.

"Follow me!" Hal invited, and led the way among the interesting centuries-old ruins.

Many of the buildings still had roofs. Some dwellings were small, while others were large and contained series of rooms, one opening into another.

"This is a huge settlement!" Louise commented. "Thousands of people must have lived here."

"That's part of what I'm trying to find out," said Hal. "I've filled several notebooks and I have a couple of theories about this place.

"The thing I must do now is establish if any of them are right. Take this spot we're coming to, for instance," he said, gesturing toward what looked to the Danas like a plaza.

"Yes?" Jean prompted with great interest.

"Well," said Hal Compton, "students don't hear so much about sacrifices among the Indians up north as they do about those of the southern Indians, especially the ones in Mexico. But I've about concluded that this section we're standing in was the centre of the city where all religious ceremonies—including sacrifices—were held. I'm trying now to determine whether animals or humans were offered to the Indian gods."

When Hal and his visitors reached the plaza, the archaeologist pointed out an enormous stone slab in the middle. Steps were carved into one side.

"This is where I think the priests—or whatever the tribe called its religious leaders—ascended with the unfortunate victim."

"Ugh!" said Jean. "It makes me shudder even to think about it."

Hal Compton laughed. "If this makes you squeamish, maybe I shouldn't show you my big discovery."

"What is it—a skeleton?" Louise asked.

"Oh, no, nothing so mild as that," the archaeologist teased. "It's the knife I figure was used in the sacrifices."

"Horrible thought!" Jean remarked, hunching her shoulders.

"Well," said Hal, "in some cultures the victims considered it an honour to be chosen as sacrificial offerings."

"Some honour! A knife in the heart!" Jean remarked, unconvinced.

The two girls and Mr. Strong followed Hal Compton to a small anteroom which he told them was part of an Indian chief's palatial home. The roof, a huge stone slab, was still intact. Inside, Hal had placed on the floor various artifacts he had found.

The young archaeologist picked up an ancient knife about ten inches long. Its blade was made of black stone.

"Isn't this magnificent?" he asked proudly.

"I suppose so," said Jean, grimacing. "But it's gruesome looking just the same."

"I'll go along with that." Hal Compton laughed

good-naturedly. "I'd say this knife is well over a thousand years old, but it still would be very effective if used today."

"I believe it," Mr. Strong remarked wryly.

Presently the group emerged into the sunshine. As they started back toward the ladder, Hal asked, "How did you all happen to be riding through here?"

"We're looking for our German shepherd dog that ran away from our train," Jean replied, and told Hal about their recent trip to the Orient, their stopover in San Francisco, and their start for home with Baron. "Have you, by any chance, seen Baron?"

"No, I haven't," Hal replied. "Sorry."

Louise asked, "Have you noticed two men riding together near here or a man and woman?"

"The answer is still no," the young man answered. "But I guess there's *someone* near here all right. While I was looking around the area, I stopped in a cave several miles back, thinking I might sleep there. But it was so far from this site that I moved out again."

Jean asked quickly, "Where was this cave?"

When Hal Compton told her, Jean and her companions were sure it was the same cave at which they had stopped.

Hal went on to say, "The place contained some interesting pictographs, which I want to go back and study. But it was littered with food, cans, and store wrappers too. The folks who left the mess couldn't have been there very long before my visit. I could tell from the date of a San Francisco newspaper they left behind."

"San Francisco!" Louise repeated thoughtfully. "Did you find anything there to identify whoever was using the cave?"

"Well, in a way, yes," Hal answered. "I suppose if I were a detective, instead of an archaeologist, I could tell you exactly who the person was. Amy tells me you girls are good sleuths. Probably you can figure this out. I saw part of a burned letter—and read it."

"What did it say?" Louise urged.

Hal Compton paused a moment to think. "Boy, you're really putting me through the third degree!" he teased. "As well as I can recall, the only words left were something like this:

'Dear Ben,
  You're letting yourself in for trouble
on this art deal. Watch that gang—'"

As the Danas exchanged startled glances, Hal Compton said in surprise, "Don't tell me you know what the letter's about!"

The young sleuths instinctively refrained from telling him their suspicions that the recipient of the letter might have been Ben Hopley.

Jean countered flippantly, "I should hope not!

Sounds as if something crooked is going on."

The sisters were thinking, nevertheless, there was a good chance that not only the letter but also the newspaper belonged to Ben Hopley. He probably had returned to the cave and discovered that both the newspaper and the letter had been moved from the spot where he had left them.

Hopley, no doubt, immediately concluded someone had been there and decided to leave at once. He had either completely destroyed the papers before the ranch group's arrival or had taken them with him.

Mr. Strong and Hal Compton now moved ahead. Louise and Jean lingered behind to discuss this possible new clue.

"Do you think Ben Hopley *is* still around?" Jean asked her sister.

"Yes, I do. He may have been the one who shot the arrow at us!"

"If he *is* that desperate, he—and his horse thief pal Simpson—must be out for big stakes!" Jean stated emphatically.

The sisters again were baffled as to what these stakes might be. Finally Louise said, "Maybe this art deal mentioned in the letter figures in the mystery. I wonder how."

Jean reminded her that Blanche Carmino had gone to art school. "If she is the witch, do you suppose that somehow she fits into the gang's scheme?"

"She could, but why is certainly a puzzle. Also, who in the gang was Ben's correspondent warning him about?"

"I have a hunch the witch will be able to answer a lot of our questions."

The girls caught up to the two men just as they reached the foot of the ladder. Hal Compton had pulled out a wallet and was scribbling his home address on a bit of paper. Finally Mr. Strong shook hands and wished the archaeologist good luck with his research.

"By the way, how did you get here?" Louise asked the Southerner.

"On a horse I rented. But he disappeared—stolen, probably."

After their own recent experiences, the girls were sure this was the case. Louise wondered if the Rineharts had taken Hal's horse too, since they could have used one.

"I've sure had bad luck with my transportation," the archaeologist went on. "A few days back I was working on a river a few miles from here. I was using a dugout somebody left, but one night it drifted away. Since then, I've had to depend on my own two feet. They're a little more reliable! When I get through with my project here, I'll just hike back to civilization!"

Mr. Strong laid a hand on Hal's shoulder. "You don't have to do that. You told me a few minutes ago you'd be winding up your work at this site in about a week. I'll come back with a horse and pick you up."

"That's right kind of you, sir." Hal smiled broadly. "Thanks. I'll be seeing you, then!"

Louise and Jean said good-by and told Hal they would like to read his thesis when it was completed.

He laughed. "You all may be old and grey by that time," he said.

The Danas and Mr. Strong went up the ladder from the pit, descended the other ladder, crossed the bench, and hurried down to their waiting horses. The riders climbed into the saddles and flicked the reins. For some time they rode along easily, then suddenly their path was blocked by a rushing stream. It was boiling with rapids, and filled with whirlpools and boulders.

The sisters were aghast. "Do we have to cross this?" Jean asked, eying the water apprehensively.

"I'm afraid we do if we expect to make it to Lost Lake," Mr. Strong replied. "There's no other way."

Louise was thoughtful. Finally she conjectured, "If someone has been trying to keep us away from Lost Lake, he probably knows about these rapids and figures we'd never follow this route. That's why we haven't been bothered since leaving the larger canyon."

"He figured wrong," Jean said. "But how are we ever going to get through this water to the other side?"

"It poses a real problem, all right," Mr. Strong said with a frown. "Suppose I walk along the bank and see if I can find a better place for us to cross."

The girls waited patiently, surveying the scene before them. The narrow gorge had suddenly ended at the stream, with level ground and a forest directly on the other side of the water.

Suddenly they heard Mr. Strong give a shout of triumph. "I've found an abandoned dugout with a paddle in it!" he said. "It must be the one Hal Compton told us had floated away."

He dragged it along the shore to where the girls were standing, then said, "I'll take the long lasso off my saddle horn, tie one end around this hooked rock, and the other to the dugout. Then I'll try to negotiate the stream in the canoe. If I have any trouble, you girls pull on the rope and bring me back."

Louise and Jean jumped from their saddles and helped to secure the dugout, while the rancher tied the other end of the rope around the rock.

"Well, here goes!" he said, stepping into the crudely made craft. "I feel like one of those old pioneers who came West."

"Or an Indian," said Jean, giggling.

The sisters held the rope, so that the dugout would not progress too fast. They could see that the going was very difficult as they watched the rancher switch his crude paddle from one side of his canoe to the other, trying to avoid the jagged rocks. The rushing water hit the craft full force, threatening to capsize it.

"Mr. Strong is amazing!" Louise said admiringly.

He was about two-thirds of the way across the raging stream when suddenly both girls cried out in alarm. Apparently the dugout had been caught in a swirling current. The canoe overturned. Mr. Strong was thrown into the water among the rocks!

CHAPTER XVII

A Perilous Crossing

As the Dana girls looked on tensely, Mr. Strong struggled amid the rapids. By this time the dugout and its paddle had been swept out of his reach. The rancher turned toward the far shore and tried to make his way there, but the swift current and slippery rocks made this impossible. He went down again!

"We must help him!" Louise said fearfully. "Jean, you pull in the dugout. I'll try to find something else to use for a paddle and go after him."

Jean hauled on the rope. The dugout moved a few inches, then stopped. It was caught on a rock. There was nothing for her to do but wait and hope that the force of the current would release it. As soon as this happened, Jean started pulling again.

"Hang on!" she cried out to Mr. Strong. "We're coming to get you as soon as we can!"

The rancher had regained his footing and stood

nearly waist-deep in the rushing water. He braced himself as best he could, and teetered as he tried to keep his balance.

"Be careful!" he shouted. "Don't let the dugout overturn again!"

Louise, meanwhile, had finally located a piece of driftwood along the shore. It was just about the right length and thickness to be used as a paddle. She picked it up and hurried back to her sister.

Slowly Jean's efforts were bringing the dugout nearer shore. There was another long wait when the craft was again caught on some protruding rocks, but eventually the rushing water freed it, and Jean was able to pull the canoe onto the bank.

"Louise, if you do manage to reach Mr. Strong in this dugout, what are you going to do then?" Jean asked.

"I'll paddle to the far shore," Louise replied. "Then, if the rope's long enough, I'll tie it to a tree over there. After that, I'll come back here in the dugout by holding onto the rope. You and I will take the horses across."

Jean heaved a tremendous sigh. "I hope it works! Good luck!"

Louise winked at her sister. "If it doesn't, a certain girl named Jean Dana may have *two* rescues on her hands!"

Jean struck a dramatic pose as if she were ready for the challenge, but instantly the two girls became serious. Louise climbed into the dugout and kneeled in the bow. She dipped her improvised paddle into the water and started across the stream.

Her sister took hold of the rope a few feet from the canoe and walked up the bank. She let out the lasso little by little as Louise battled the current. Fortunately, her skill, together with Jean's perfect timing, manoeuvred the craft so that it came alongside Mr. Strong.

"I won't climb in," he said, gasping. "I'll just hold on to the dugout and guide it. Keep going, Louise. You're doing a swell job."

By this time Louise was too far out in the stream for Jean to be of much service except to hold onto the rope. She held her breath at each dip of Louise's paddle. But finally the two reached the opposite shore in safety. The rope had proved to be long enough.

"Hurray!" Jean cried out.

Louise and Mr. Strong waved their thanks for her part in the rescue, then the rancher said, "If we expect to continue our journey, the hardest part is yet to come. We'll have to figure out how to bring Jean and the horses across."

Louise smiled. "I have an idea," she said, and told him what she had in mind.

"That's fine—just fine," he approved. "Wish I could be of more help, but I think I'd better rest for a while. I'm all in."

His legs were almost numb from the ice-cold water and the pounding of the turbulent stream, the rancher confessed. He also had bruises and abrasions on his face and hands, and was very pale.

Mr. Strong rolled up his wet trousers, took off his boots and socks, and chafed his legs vigorously. Louise asked him if there was anything she could do to make him more comfortable, but he told her:

"Don't worry. Just concentrate on getting Jean and the horses to this side of the water."

She untied the end of the rope from the dugout and secured it tightly to a tree limb. The ample line was nearly taut, exactly the way she wanted it.

Louise gripped the dugout, pushed it back into the water, and stepped aboard. She swung her right arm over the guide rope, then began to paddle toward the opposite shore. The journey back was not easy, but with the aid of the rope she found it to be less arduous than the trip over.

When she reached her sister, Jean whooped for joy. "You're marvellous!" she shouted. "Absolutely marvellous!"

"Better save your praise until we and the horses are on the other side," Louise cautioned.

"I think we should loop each horse's reins around the rope and tie the lines together," Jean suggested.

"But we're short of rope."

"How about our belts?" Jean asked.

"Fine," Louise agreed.

The two girls whipped off their leather belts. Louise tied hers from Ginger's back saddle string to the bridle rings of Silver Streak, while Jean tied hers from Silver Streak to Jubilee. She herself would hold the lead rope of the pack horse.

Louise mounted and led the way, looping her reins across the lasso and tying them. Jean swung Silver Streak's lines over the rope and secured them to the saddle horn. Finally she mounted Jubilee, adjusted her reins, tossed the lead rope over the lasso, and held it firmly.

"All set?" Louise called. "Let's go!"

The sisters held onto the lasso with one hand, and with the other, the manes of their horses. They guided the animals with their knees, in and out among the boulders. Both girls knew the horses could easily slip and break a leg. The rope swayed back and forth, and once it was pulled so tightly when the pack horse stumbled that the girls were afraid it might snap in two. But the lasso held.

Mr. Strong watched the scene with bated breath. How brave the girls were, he thought! And how resourceful!

When the girls reached the precarious spot where the rancher had gone overboard, they became especially cautious. Once Ginger faltered, and Louise's heart gave a leap. But the mare kept her balance and went on, plodding at a very slow rate through the water.

Finally the palomino reached the bank with Silver Streak directly behind her. In a few moments Jean, Jubilee, and the pack horse were safe.

Mr. Strong wrung the girls' hands warmly. "I never thought you could do it!" he said. "When you were halfway across, I was kicking myself for allowing you even to try it."

Louise and Jean laughed, and Jean said, "Maybe we should thank Hal Compton for that dugout. Without it, we might still be stranded on the other side! By the way, who's going back to untie the other end of this lasso and bring it here?"

"I think," said Mr. Strong, "that we ought to leave the rope the way it is. We may want to get back across in a hurry!"

It suddenly occurred to the three adventurers that they were extremely hungry. Mr. Strong, feeling that everyone had had enough exercise for the day, including the horses, said:

"I suggest that we make camp here for the night. It's a good level spot."

The day had turned out to be an unseasonably warm one, and the girls were sure they would enjoy sleeping outside. Mr. Strong asked them to gather wood for a small fire, which he would let burn until daylight.

Louise looked at him worriedly. "To keep away wild animals, I suppose?" she asked.

The rancher nodded. "I'm not taking any more chances," he said. "We've been lucky so far. We mustn't tempt fate."

The Danas opened cans of meat, beans, and tomato juice, then the campers gathered around the fire. As they ate, Mr. Strong began to tell stories of his life in the West.

Jean's eyes had wandered toward the horses. Presently she asked, "Silver Streak is so beautiful! Where did you get him?"

Proudly the rancher said that he had caught the horse himself. "He was just a little fellow—one of a band of wild horses. He was as frisky as they come, right from the start. Getting a hackamore on him was like doing a fast-stepping dance."

"And how about the saddle?" Louise asked.

"That was even worse," Mr. Strong replied. "I thought I'd never get that colt broken to the saddle. But you know, once it was accomplished, he became gentler and more responsive than most horses. I wouldn't part with him for all the gold in Colorado—at least I don't *think* I would," he added with a grin.

Soon dusk came on and the three weary travellers unrolled their sleeping bags. As the Danas nestled into theirs, the girls' thoughts turned to Baron. Where was he? Would they ever see him again, alive and safe? Despite these troubled thoughts, they drifted off to sleep.

It was morning when they awakened. The sisters looked around. Mr. Strong was nowhere in sight.

"I wonder where he went," said Jean, crawling out of her bag.

"Maybe he went off to get wood for a breakfast fire," Louise guessed.

The girls rolled up their sleeping bags and put them on the pack horse. Then they washed at the stream, and combed their hair. Still Mr. Strong did not appear.

"Oh, dear, I hope nothing has happened to him," said Louise, and called the rancher's name loudly several times.

There was no answer.

CHAPTER XVIII

Treed Detectives

"WHERE can Mr. Strong be?" Louise said worriedly.

Jean was equally alarmed. She could think of no reason why the rancher should have gone very far from camp. Had something happened to him?

"We should look for footprints," Louise suggested. "Maybe Ben Hopley or Chet Simpson or the Rineharts came sneaking around here! Mr. Strong may have gone after them and was captured!"

"And they left us alone because those men figured we couldn't get far without him," Jean surmised.

Louise was already looking along the shore for boot prints. Hearing a sound from the forest, she looked up quickly, then gave a little scream.

"Jean! A bear!"

Her sister looked ahead in horror. Loping toward them was a large black bear!

"We'd better climb a tree—and quick!" Jean advised.

"But bears can climb trees, too!" Louise countered despairingly. "He'll come right after us!"

"We'll each take a tree," Jean said. "He can't chase both of us at once."

"You're right."

Quickly each girl shinned up a pine tree and swung onto the lowest branch. At the same time, the bear came sniffing at the tree where Jean had taken refuge. Suddenly, apparently getting the aroma of their food supply, he turned and lumbered toward the provisions.

"Good!" Jean exclaimed. "He's going to have breakfast. That'll keep him busy—he may forget all about us."

Louise groaned. "But if he eats everything up, we'll starve!"

"I'd rather starve than be his food supply!" Jean answered.

The sisters watched while the beast tore open packages of bacon and smashed cans against a rock with his great paw. As chicken soup spilled out over the ground he licked it up hungrily.

The Danas were dismayed when the attacker moved away and once more came toward them.

Jean said, "I'll bet he's disappointed not to find

anything sweet. Well, I feel good and sour. Maybe he won't bother me!"

The bear walked to the tree in which Louise was perched, wound his forepaws around the trunk, and began to climb. Louise, in panic, scrambled up into the higher branches.

Jean broke off several branches and desperately threw them in the bear's direction. He paid no attention. Next, she took off a boot and flung this at the animal. It hit him in the back, making him turn around for a moment. Then he continued his climb.

Louise was now high in the tree but with a sinking heart she watched the bear's ascent. The girl fought down a wave of terror. In minutes those great claws would reach out for her!

"I must stop him!" Jean was thinking wildly.

As she was trying to figure out how, a shot suddenly rang out! There was a slight humming sound, then a bullet landed in the tree trunk just above the bear's nose!

The animal, frightened, dropped back to the ground and scuttled away. In a moment Mr. Strong appeared from among the trees, carrying his rifle.

"Guess I got back just in time," he said with a chuckle. "Being treed by a bear is no fun."

"I agree!" said Louise, as she made her way down the trunk. "Thanks a million!"

"We've really had *two* frights," Jean told him.

"First, we were terribly concerned about you—we thought you might have had an accident or even been captured."

"I'm sorry to have worried you," the rancher said. "When you hear my story you'll have a chance to laugh at what happened to me."

Mr. Strong explained that he had awakened early and gone to find the Stetson hat he had lost when he was thrown out of the dugout.

"My head sure felt bare without it," he added. "I found the hat on the shore about a quarter of a mile down from where we landed, and then started back. Just before I reached camp, all of a sudden this same bear appeared and treed me!

"I heard you girls call, but I didn't answer on purpose. I hoped old bruin would annoy me until he got tired and then leave, without bothering you. As it turns out he did exactly what I hoped he wouldn't, so I climbed down and trailed him."

"You could have shot him, but you didn't," Louise remarked.

"No," said Mr. Strong, "I don't believe in killing wild animals unless it's necessary. I figure they have as much right to this territory as I do—maybe even more. It's only when one attacks first that I use my rifle."

"Well, I certainly hope you scared him off for good!" Jean said fervently.

The travellers cleaned their camp, ate breakfast,

then carried the remaining supplies to the pack horse and saddled up.

They rode for about an hour, part of the time through canyon country. Finally they came out onto a large flat bench.

Mr. Strong called a halt and said, "From the end of this bench we should be able to see what is left of Lost Lake."

"I'm so excited," said Jean, "I can hardly wait!"

"Will we ride down there?" Louise asked, her own pulses quickening.

"Not yet," the rancher replied. "We'll hitch our horses to this natural rock post and walk over to the edge."

Quickly the sisters dismounted and tied Ginger and Jubilee. Then they hurried ahead of Mr. Strong toward the rim of the bench. Reaching it, they gazed in awe at the panorama below.

In the background was a small greenish-blue lake, which drained into a tiny river. From the near end of the lake a steep, craggy mountain rose at a precipitous angle. The girls' eyes finally focused on the small level stretch of foreground near the base of the mountain.

Jean clutched Louise's arm. *"The witch!"* she whispered, gazing at a woman standing there.

Louise said tensely, "You're right, Jean. She must be the witch of Lost Lake!"

CHAPTER XIX

Prisoners!

THE woman at the foot of the cliff was dressed in trousers, a jacket, and wore a man's felt hat pushed back on her head. Straight grey hair streamed to her waist. She was digging.

Some little distance away was a tiny log cabin, built near the foot of the mountain. Alongside it an Appaloosa pony was tethered.

"This woman doesn't *look* like a witch," Louise said finally. "She's actually pretty, and she has a very sweet face."

By this time Mr. Strong had joined the Danas. He looked down and blinked in astonishment.

"The story about the witch *was* true," he said. "The strange woman does live here!"

"But she doesn't seem like a witch," Louise insisted. "She looks very kind."

"Don't forget, she has a reputation for being handy with a gun," Mr. Strong reminded the girls.

"I see she has a rifle lying right alongside her."

"I'm going to speak to the woman, anyway," Louise said resolutely. "We promised ourselves we'd try to help her."

"All right, but be careful," the rancher advised. "I suggest we all lie on our stomachs and peek over the bench, so if she does take a potshot at us we can duck."

The three got down and peered over the edge. In a friendly tone, Louise called, "Hello, Miss Carmino!"

The woman gave a start and looked up. At the same time she grabbed her rifle, ready for action.

"Please put down your gun," Jean requested. "We're not going to bother or harm you. Aren't you Miss Blanche Carmino?"

The stranger did not answer the question, but in a low, cultured voice she said, "I never hurt a friend. Who are you?"

The Danas and Mr. Strong stood up. Louise went on, "We want to be your friends. We're two sisters from the East, hunting for our dog which is lost in these mountains. This kind rancher has been guiding us on our search."

Jean added, "Our dog is a beautiful German shepherd. We thought he might have headed in this direction."

"Tell me more about him," the woman said.

The girls described Baron Otto von Neckar. Then they introduced themselves and Mr. Strong.

When the lone inhabitant of Lost Lake did not answer, the rancher gave her a big reassuring grin. "You might say we're neighbours—even though some distance apart," he observed, "so we certainly would like to know how to address you properly."

Suddenly she laughed in a musical voice. "Yes, I am Blanche Carmino. Please come down. I would like to talk to you."

Delighted, the trio slid down the sloping rocky wall until they reached the foot, then walked across the open space to where Miss Carmino had been digging.

When they reached her, she shook hands with each of her callers. "Follow me!" she suggested, and headed toward the cabin.

They had barely started, when from the back of the small building came a joyful bark. Louise and Jean, excited, started to run. They rounded the corner of the building and gave cries of delight.

"Baron!" they shouted. "We've found you!"

The dog appeared to be in fine condition. He leaped about, straining at the chain which held him fast. He wagged his tail furiously and kept on barking. Louise and Jean took turns hugging the German shepherd, who seemed as glad to see them as they were to see him.

Mr. Strong and Miss Carmino stood in the background, smiling. Finally the woman said, "If I had any misgivings about the dog's being yours, I do not have them now."

"How long has Baron been here?" Louise asked.

"Actually he has been here twice," the woman replied. "The first time was about a week ago. He seemed absolutely exhausted. I fed him and he slept soundly for hours. Baron is so beautiful I was hoping he would stay, but he disappeared. I was greatly worried."

The Danas nodded understandingly. "We know how you felt," said Jean. "When did Baron return, Miss Carmino?"

"The day before yesterday. What a relief to see him safe and unhurt! This time I had a feeling he must be somebody's pet and was lost. I decided to keep him until the next time I went to town, intending to take him along and turn him over to the deputy sheriff."

"It's certainly lucky for us," said Jean, "that you decided to keep him."

She then told Miss Carmino about the train wreck and how the dog had disappeared. "Our Aunt Harriet will certainly be happy to see Baron."

"Yes," Louise put in. "You see, he's a valuable show dog, and we're taking him to New York to his new owner. We would have felt terrible at having to break the news that we had lost Baron."

The woman's face took on a worried expression.

"I should tell you something else, girls," she said. "Twice in the past two days people have tried to steal him."

Excitedly the Danas and Mr. Strong pressed for details.

"First," Blanche Carmino continued, "two men came sneaking in here night before last. Baron barked loudly and I went out. When I saw the men going toward him, I shot my rifle into the air and it scared them off."

"But they returned?" Jean guessed.

"No," replied Miss Carmino. "Yesterday a man and a woman came." Seeing the Danas and Mr. Strong exchange glances, she asked if they knew the couple.

"We're not sure," Louise answered. "But we've met four suspicious people in the mountains that could be the ones who tried to steal Baron."

Suddenly Miss Carmino glanced at Mr. Strong, who had a somewhat quizzical expression on his face. She smiled charmingly and shrugged her shoulders.

"I can see that you think I'm not telling everything."

The rancher started to apologize, but she went on cordially, "Please, everyone, come inside the cabin and I will tell you my whole story."

Louise and Jean were thrilled. Perhaps at last they were going to learn the secret of Lost Lake!

"Thanks. We'd like to," said Mr. Strong.

Miss Carmino led them to the front of the cabin. She opened the door to reveal a charming interior. The cozy living-sleeping quarters were filled with artistic handmade rustic furniture. In one corner stood an easel with a half-finished landscape painting on it. The walls were filled with unframed pastels and water colours of the surrounding scenery and of wild animals.

"We heard you once studied at art school," Louise remarked. "Are all these lovely drawings yours?"

As Miss Carmino nodded, Jean commented, "They're marvellous! Do you ever sell your work?"

Miss Carmino smiled a bit sadly. "I tried to when I visited in New York many years ago, but didn't find any customers. I guess I'd been away from city life too long. It was difficult for me to meet people."

She invited her sympathetic listeners to be seated, then continued, "You doubtless have heard of the great earthquake and landslide that devastated this region forty years ago."

"Yes, we have," Jean said, leaning forward in her eagerness to hear Blanche Carmino's next words.

"Well"—their hostess gave a tremulous sigh—"that disaster changed my whole life so suddenly that it hasn't been until recent years I've felt somewhat recovered from the shock."

The artist related the sad account of her parents' death. "For a time my health was broken completely. I just wanted to live here alone and had sufficient money. After a while I began painting pictures, building this furniture, and digging for artifacts. This seemed to help me."

"Did you build the cabin too?" Jean asked.

"No, that was here. The only building left in town. No one was here, so I claimed it."

The interesting woman went on to say that the Danas and Mr. Strong were the only friendly people she had met in years. The shopkeepers in Huntersville were barely civil to her, and certain impolite people in town annoyed her whenever she went for supplies.

Jean diplomatically changed the subject. Recalling that Aunt Harriet had heard of an Antonio Carmino, she took a chance and asked, "Your father, Antonio, was a famous man, wasn't he?"

Blanche looked at Jean in amazement. "Yes, he was—that is—in his own field. But how did you know?"

Jean grinned and explained Miss Dana's familiarity with Carmino's name. "But we still don't know what your father did or why he came to Pueblo Lake."

"Then I will tell you." The artist said that she and her mother and father once lived in New York City. Antonio Carmino was a sculptor of note, but his health had become very poor and the doctor had ordered him to move out into the clear, dry air of the Rocky Mountains.

"Father chose Pueblo Lake because it was so picturesque," she went on. "But directly after we arrived, he learned that people in town, although good-hearted, were the hard-working, rugged, practical type and had no use for artists of any kind."

She said that in order to avoid gossip, her father had done his sculpting in a secluded cave. "There's some very fine variegated coloured rock in this mountain which he used for his statues."

Ever since the group had entered the cabin, Baron had been barking almost continuously. Miss Carmino smiled. "I guess the dog wants to be with you. I'll unchain Baron and bring him inside."

The artist returned in a few moments with the dog and closed the door.

"We'll have tea while we talk," she told her guests, and went into a small adjoining room that evidently served as a kitchen.

While water was boiling for the tea, she carried in an exquisitely decorated flower tray on which was a tea service of very fine china. Furthermore, the misnamed witch had combed her hair and arranged it gracefully on top of her head. She really looked very attractive, the Danas observed.

"You people make me feel like my old self, and using this china I brought from New York is fun," Miss Carmino said, giggling almost girlishly. She served the fragrant tea and some home-baked cookies.

"Would you like to hear more of my story?" the artist asked, as they sipped the beverage.

"Yes, indeed!" Louise replied, at the same time patting Baron who had stretched out at her feet.

Miss Carmino went on, "The people who tried to steal Baron are after another big prize. Somehow they found out about my buried secret and want to locate it themselves."

Louise and Jean put down their teacups. Both were in a state of suspense and eagerness to hear at last the details of the mysterious area.

"Those people—I don't know their names— have come here several times. The couple offered money if I would disclose the statues' hiding place. The two men threatened to harm me unless I do. But I *never* will tell any of them!

"But I *will* tell you. At the time of the great landslide and the death of everyone here, I knew from a letter of Mother's that my father had finished several very fine statues. They were in the cave he used as a studio. That is the treasure spot these dreadful men want me to tell them about, so they can steal and sell the masterpieces."

"What an amazing story!" said Louise. "Is the cave nearby?"

Miss Carmino sighed. "That's the trouble. I don't know where it is because the landslide buried so many familiar landmarks. For years after I returned here, I was not equal to searching for the statues. Finally I regained enough strength to start digging—first for the Indian artifacts and later to locate the cave."

"That must have seemed an impossible task," Jean remarked.

"It did, for a long time," Blanche Carmino admitted. "And I had to be constantly on guard against snooping people from this area. And then one can't do much digging in the long winters or during heavy rains."

The artist went on to say she had recently uncovered some sculpting tools that she knew had belonged to her father. "He must have dropped them as he raced for home. They gave me a wonderful clue to the cave's whereabouts." Miss Carmino's face clouded over. "Then those unscrupulous men came along. I'm afraid to do more digging now."

Excitedly the Danas inquired what she thought was the buried studio's location.

"I believe the cave is just at the point where the lake makes a southwest bend. You can't see it from here. My father's studio was so well protected that I am sure his statues are intact."

"Oh, how I'd love to help you find them!" said Jean.

Mr. Strong, being more practical, suggested that

Miss Carmino tell her story to the authorities, stake a claim on the property, and then have trained people do the digging.

"It's a fine idea," Miss Carmino agreed, "but I wouldn't have enough money to pay them. It has always been my idea that if I could locate the cave and see if there's anything inside, then I'd get help."

Jean was excited. "Please let us help you dig!"

"All right," said Miss Carmino, who flushed in anticipation. "I'll show you the way."

She led the group to the door and gave it a pull. To her amazement, the door would not open.

"This is strange," she said, giving the handle another yank.

Mr. Strong stepped forward and offered his help. The door still would not budge.

Louise, instantly suspicious the door might have been barred by someone on the outside, dashed to a window. She looked out and exclaimed, "There's a man with a rifle! He's pointing it this way! I can't see his face—his hat's pulled way down."

The others ran to her side. One glance, and they had no doubt now as to what had happened. They were prisoners! One or more men had quietly sneaked up and probably secured the door handle with a rope in such a way that the door could not be pulled open from the inside.

"That low-down crook is not going to get away

with this!" Mr. Strong exclaimed angrily. "I'll go out the window after him!"

Miss Carmino cried out, "No! I won't let you risk your life and that of these girls for my sake. If anyone goes out, I'll be the one!"

Suddenly, from the other side of the door, came a loud, self-satisfied laugh. Then a man called loudly:

"No one better come out, if you value your lives! Don't make any trouble, and we'll leave you alone. Thanks to the witch, we know where Antonio Carmino's statues are! After we dig them out and take the treasures away, you can leave the cabin, but not before!"

CHAPTER XX

A Grateful Witch

AFTER the first outburst of anger by Miss Carmino and Mr. Strong, there was silence in the besieged cabin. Louise and Jean felt responsible for the imprisonment of the four, since it was the sisters' search for Baron that had brought them to Lost Lake. For the moment the Danas were nonplused —how could they figure out a means of escape?

Baron broke the silence by barking loudly. He bounded over and placed his paws against the door, as if to frighten the men or to signal that he wanted to go outside and fight them.

"No, Baron," said Mr. Strong. "You'd be shot in a minute even if we could let you out." He paced the floor. "Why, oh why did I ever allow you girls to get into this predicament?"

Louise and Jean looked out the window again at the man holding the rifle. This time his hat was pushed back and he had lowered his weapon.

Now Louise exclaimed, "It's Sam Rinehart!"

"And I think," Jean added, "that the man outside the door is Ben Hopley. I believe he was trying to disguise his voice but it still sounded like his."

Miss Carmino spoke up in a whisper. "Perhaps if we wait until evening, I can slip out the window and go for help."

Mr. Strong shook his head vigorously. "That will be my job!"

Jean reminded the others that darkness was a long way off. It was just possible that their captors had a whole gang of men already digging at the site of the landslide. "Too bad we didn't hear them sneak up when we were talking about the hidden cave."

Blanche Carmino groaned, then set her jaw firmly. "They must not find it!" she said. "I'm going to stop those men if I have to—"

Before she could finish the sentence, a series of shots rang out on the mountainside. The group in the cabin was mystified. Were the thieves having a fight among themselves?

A moment later a loud, stern voice commanded, *"Put up your hands!"*

The Danas rushed to the window and were just in time to see several deputy sheriffs ride in on horseback. Among them was Deputy Alt.

In a short time they had rounded up Sam Rinehart and Ben Hopley, then Chet Simpson and

Sally Rinehart who had already started digging.

As soon as the rifles of the three men had been taken from them and the rope-tie cut from the door, Louise and Jean rushed from the cabin with Miss Carmino, Mr. Strong, and Baron. The girls spoke at once to Deputy Alt.

"So you *have* been prisoners!" he said. "Your aunt was afraid that might happen."

"Our Aunt Harriet?" Louise gasped.

"Yes," said the deputy sheriff. "She suddenly recalled that Antonio Carmino had been a famous sculptor. She guessed then that the secret of Lost Lake might concern work of his buried here. If so, and the horse thieves were after it, they might take any kind of measures to keep you away from this spot."

"And they did!" Jean exclaimed.

"I can't wait to thank Aunt Harriet," said Louise. "She really came to our rescue. By the way, this is our missing dog."

"You found him! Great!"

The deputy sheriff advised the prisoners of their rights and that they did not have to answer any questions. They chose to reveal everything that had happened.

Ben Hopley was a self-styled artist and sculptor but had never been able to make an honest living at his profession. He had resorted to stealing anything he could sell.

Chet Simpson turned out to be an agent for art dealers with shady reputations. Mrs. Rinehart was his sister. Her husband, who proved to be the real brains of the outfit, had come across a clue in New York City that some valuable works of Antonio Carmino might be buried at Lost Lake.

Miss Carmino identified Hopley and Simpson as the men who had tried to steal Baron and had threatened her if she did not reveal her secret. She explained that the Rineharts were involved in both nefarious schemes.

"I'm glad we got here before they carried out their plans," Deputy Alt replied. He turned to the Danas. "This has been a challenging mystery for you girls. Would you like to ask the prisoners any questions?"

Louise nodded and spoke to Ben Hopley. "Were you the one who carved the petroglyph of the old woman with the man sneaking up behind her, planning to knock her out with a shovel?"

"Yes, I did it at Rinehart's instructions. Chet and I were casing this territory. Sam and Sally were waiting. They told us that when no one was around and everything was ready for them to close in on the witch, I was to chip out that petroglyph as a signal. Then you butted in."

"Who," Jean asked, "spoke those mysterious words, 'Get the witch!' and 'Beautiful artwork'?"

Startled, the thieves looked at one another

before answering, but finally Sally Rinehart spoke up. "Sam did. I didn't know anybody could hear us!"

"There's an echoing rock wall," said Louise. "It proved to be a good clue for us. How about the cabin where we found you?"

"We were all set up at that cabin—stocked it and even brought kerosene lanterns—to masquerade as lost hunters. Then you had to come barging in. You've been the cause of nothing but trouble for us."

Sam Rinehart confessed they had planned to steal all three horses so that Mr. Strong and the girls would have to trek home. "But you were too quick for us," he told the rancher, hatred in his eyes.

Louise and Jean learned that the Rineharts had driven from New York in their car. They had kept it hidden a good part of the time in a box canyon outside of Huntersville. They had used the stolen ranch horses when travelling through the mountains.

"Did you also steal a horse from an archaeologist working in the ruined Indian cliff dwellings?" Louise queried.

"Yes," Rinehart answered. "You'll find all of them at Round Table Butte. But it was Simpson who was spying on you and let you see him. Pretty dumb!"

The remark angered Chet Simpson. "*Me* dumb!" he cried out. "You were a fool to call out a fake warning to the girls and Mr. Strong in that canyon and then shoot an arrow. You sure alerted them."

It was further revealed by the thieves that Hopley and Simpson had formerly lived in New York but now were residents of San Francisco. They knew the Lost Lake area thoroughly from various trips to it. They usually used stolen horses in their travels.

Ben Hopley had stayed in the cave and had lost a letter from a friend warning him about the Rineharts. He and Simpson had separated—Chet to trail the ranch group, and Ben Hopley to go ahead and try to scare them into turning back.

All the prisoners had been handcuffed and now Deputy Alt was ready to have them mount horses and be taken to jail.

Louise stepped forward. "Sir," she said, "you have so many men here, couldn't all of us take a little time to dig and try to find the buried statues?"

The deputy sheriff seemed a bit startled by this request. Before he could answer, Miss Carmino, whose eyes were sparkling with excitement, said quickly, "I have plenty of picks and shovels and spades if you could possibly spare the time."

Suddenly the law officer laughed. "I think it's a splendid idea," he said to Louise.

Deputy Sheriff Alt appointed one of his men to

stand guard while the group followed Miss Carmino to the spot where she thought her father's cave workshop had been.

Blanche Carmino suggested that they dig in a circular area about five feet apart. Fifteen minutes went by with no success, then thirty. Mr. Strong called out, "I think we should take a rest period."

"Wait a second!" Jean cried excitedly. "Louise and I have just struck something!"

The others rushed to the spot. Before they could reach the girls, a wooden door which the sisters had uncovered suddenly gave way at their feet. The Danas disappeared, as if swallowed up by the earth!

Mr. Strong was terrified. He leaned over and peered into the yawning hole. "Louise! Jean!" he called. "Where are you? Are you all right?"

"We're okay," Louise called back, to everyone's relief. "Please throw down a flashlight!"

The rancher got one from his saddlebag and dropped it into the pit. Louise turned on the beam and flashed it around.

The sisters found that they had tumbled into a tunnel. Now it began to ascend abruptly. Together, the girls walked forward. Suddenly they stopped. The powerful light revealed a rock-walled cavern untouched by the landslide and preserved intact.

"Look!" Jean cried.

Ahead of the girls were five exquisitely carved

statues. Two were still standing, three lying on the floor of the cave.

"They *are* priceless!" Louise said in awe as she gazed at the figures of an Indian and a graceful antelope.

Hurrying back to the doorway, the sisters reported their find. At once Miss Carmino entered the cave, followed by Mr. Strong and several of the deputy sheriff's men. All gazed in admiration at Antonio Carmino's work, so long hidden from the world.

Tears trickled down the cheeks of his daughter. "My father was a wonderful man and a great sculptor," she said. "His work should be displayed in museums so everyone can appreciate it. I will take these statues to New York and sell them."

Louise and Jean clasped her hands and smiled. "And you will stay in New York yourself and have some fun, won't you?" Jean said.

The artist looked at the sisters affectionately. "You girls have taught me a great lesson. I have wasted many years being a recluse. But now I shall try to make up for it. I want to prove to everyone here that I never have been a witch. I was a broken-hearted person afraid of the world. You girls have restored my confidence."

The group walked back through the tunnel that led from the cave. Only Deputy Sheriff Alt and two other men remained. He said the prisoners had already been taken away.

"These men will stay here to guard the statues until they can be safely moved," he assured Miss Carmino.

The Danas, though happy at the way everything had turned out, could not help but wonder if another mystery might come their way. It would, and soon—*The Winking Ruby Mystery*.

All this time, Baron had been frisking about. Louise and Jean realized that momentarily they had forgotten about him. It was fortunate for them that he had not run off again!

Louise gave the dog a hug. "I guess you've had enough scares in these mountains and won't mind staying aboard the train to New York," she teased him.

As Baron Otto von Neckar wagged his tail furiously and barked in response, Jean said, "Do you know, old fellow, it was really you who solved the secret of Lost Lake. It's just too bad you can't tell us one word about *your* adventures!"

Louise laughed. "We must send a telegram to Professor Nesbitt and say, 'Mission accomplished'!"

The Sparrow Bookshop

Sparrow has a whole nestful of exciting books that are available in bookshops or that you can order by post through the Sparrow Bookshop. Just complete the form below and enclose the money due and the books will be sent to you at home.

THE MYSTERY OF THE STONE TIGER	Carolyn Keene	95p	☐
THE PONY SEEKERS	D. Pullein-Thompson	95p	☐
THE NO-GOOD PONY	J. Pullein-Thompson	95p	☐
FLY-BY-NIGHT	K. M. Peyton	95p	☐
THE NEW TV SERIES OF WORZEL GUMMIDGE AND AUNT SALLY	Waterhouse and Hall	90p	☐
WORZEL GUMMIDGE AND THE TREASURE SHIP	B. E. Todd	95p	☐
RICHARD BOLITHO – MIDSHIPMAN	Alexander Kent	95p	☐
THE SPUDDY	Lillian Beckwith	85p	☐
AGAINST THE SEA	Douglas Reeman	95p	☐

Humour

LAUGH-A-MINUTE JOKE BOOK	Paul James	90p	☐
JELLYBONE GRAFITTI BOOK	Therese Birch	85p	☐
COMPLETE PRACTICAL JOKER	Peter Eldin	95p	☐
NEVER WEAR YOUR WELLIES IN THE HOUSE	Tom Baker	85p	☐

Total plus postage

And if you would like to hear more about our forthcoming books, write to the address below for the Sparrow News.

SPARROW BOOKS, BOOKSERVICE BY POST, PO BOX 29, DOUGLAS, ISLE OF MAN, BRITISH ISLES

Please enclose a cheque or postal order made out to Arrow Books Limited for the amount due including 8p per book for postage and packing for orders within the UK and 10p for overseas orders.

Please print clearly

NAME _____

ADDRESS _____

_____

Whilst every effort is made to keep prices down and popular books in print, Arrow Books cannot guarantee that prices will be the same as those advertised here or that the books will be available.